DARE TO RESIST

BARBARA RAE ROBINSON

Contact at barbararae@gmail.com

Cover design by Christy Keerins

Dare to Resist / Barbara Rae Robinson

First edition

EBOOK ISBN: 978-0-9971824-0-8

PRINT ISBN: 978-0-9971824-1-5

❀ Created with Vellum

This book is dedicated to my husband, Jim,
for his patience over the years as I pursued my dream,
and to my Romex sisters for their continuing support, especially the
Pursuit gang.

CHAPTER 1

*T*ricia Landreth juggled her briefcase and purse and stabbed the key into the lock. It wouldn't turn. She squinted at her keys, but the dim light from the street lamps didn't penetrate the shadows of her front porch.

"Damn it." She closed her eyes, then opened them again. This is all I need after being accused of messing up the spreadsheet so it doesn't balance.

She tried the next key. After fumbling a bit, she found the keyhole. She took a couple of deep breaths. The long day and the tension-filled dinner meeting had sapped her strength.

Focus. Focus. This time the key turned and the deadbolt clicked open. One more lock. Taking her time, she inserted the other key into the door lock, leaned heavily on the door, and stumbled inside. She bumped the front door closed with her hip, flipped the bolt, and snapped on the living room light.

Cigarette smoke. A lingering odor. The type that follows a heavy smoker when they walk through a room.

Her simmering anger flared. "Damn them." The cleaning

service must have sent a smoker again after she'd told them not to. Tomorrow she'd start her search for another service. She shoved her keys into her purse and massaged her forehead.

Tonight she'd relax in her big tub and soak away the frustrations of her long day.

Tomorrow she'd deal with the problems at work.

She plodded up the stairs, dropped her purse and briefcase on the bed, and stepped into her bathroom.

On the mirror, scrawled in red lipstick, a stark message. *You are mine! Then you die!*

An icy chill spiraled down her spine. She crept closer and read the words again.

That icy chill erupted into full blown panic. Shaking her arms, her shoulders, her whole body.

She stumbled against the wall. Stared at the hateful words. And concentrated on staying upright. *Think. Think.*

Whoever sent her those two notes had been inside her house. Inside her bedroom. Her gaze darted around the room.

Was he still in the house?

She held her breath, listening for sounds. All she could hear was her own escalating heartbeat. The pound, pound, pound echoing in her ears. *Gotta get out of the house. Gotta call the police.*

She snagged her purse off the bed and ran down the stairs as fast as she dared in high heels. Ran through the door, down the steps, and through the gate to the sidewalk.

Ignoring the light Oregon rain, she fumbled in her purse for her cell phone. Keeping an eye on the open front door, she called 911, and gave the dispatcher her name and address. Then added, "My house was locked. But someone has been inside. I don't know if he's hiding somewhere in the house."

"Where are you now?" The dispatcher's voice was calm and controlled.

"Outside. On the sidewalk." She looked both ways and couldn't see anyone else nearby at this late hour. A few cars traveled the commercial street a half block away. But no cars passed by on her residential street. Her usually bustling neighborhood was eerily quiet. She shivered.

"Are you safe where you are?" The compassionate voice helped.

"I don't know. I'll wait for the police in my car."

"Don't hang up until the police arrive, and stay in your car until they tell you to get out."

"Okay." She'd parked her car on the paved strip to the right of the front yard fence. She grabbed her keys from her purse, unlocked the driver door, and scrambled inside out of the cold October rain. Her heart hammered against her chest wall. She pushed the door lock. "I'm in my car."

"I'll stay on the line until the police get there and take over."

"Okay."

A car drove by, going slow. Tricia ducked down, as low as she could, and hugged the console so tight her arms ached.

THE SHRILL SHRIEK of a siren split the air. Headlights streamed through the darkness, then a patrol car careened to the curb in front of the house. The officer sprinted to her car and tapped on the glass. Tricia rolled down the window.

"Are you Tricia Landreth?"

"Yes."

The officer flashed his ID. "Officer Shawn Murray, Portland Police Bureau. What happened?"

"A man was in my house. I came home. Found his note. He

plans to kill me. I don't know how he got in." Her words spilled out, slurred together.

"Is he still there?" The officer studied her as if assessing her mental state. "Did you see him?"

"No. I only saw his message. I got out fast." She slowed her speech, to appear more coherent.

"You told the dispatcher the door was locked when you got home."

"Yes. Double-locked. With a dead bolt." Waves of disbelief rushed through her. This couldn't be happening.

"We'll check out the house." He stepped back from her car and radioed for backup.

The officer finished his call and came back to her window. "Lock up your car and come over to the patrol car."

As she got out of her car, she jerked up the hood of her coat to ward off the now heavier rain. He escorted her to the patrol car and opened the back passenger door. She scooted onto the seat and he stood by the door, leaving it ajar.

"Okay, tell me from the beginning. What happened?" He watched the house instead of her.

Tricia glanced at the open door and took a shuddering breath. "I came home late and headed straight upstairs to the bathroom to start the water for a bath. I saw what he wrote on the mirror, so I ran downstairs and outside." She rushed the words, as if telling her story fast made it less real.

"What did he write?"

"You are mine, then you die." She repeated the awful words, and that icy chill gripped her. Settled inside her so deep she doubted she'd ever be warm.

The officer's expression remained neutral. "Do you know who wrote it?"

"I...I think I have a stalker." She pulled her coat tighter and clutched her purse to her chest.

"Have you reported this stalker?"

"No. I wasn't sure. But I've received two unsigned notes in the mail over the past two weeks. They both said, 'You're mine.'"

"We'll get you some help." Officer Murray was an older man, and matter-of-fact and business-like. That helped her calm down.

Maybe something could be done. The problems at work were enough, without a scary stalker. Was a boring and normal life too much to ask for?

Another siren signaled the arrival of a second patrol car. Another uniformed officer joined them on the sidewalk.

Then a third patrol car arrived with two more officers. "What do we have?" one officer asked.

"Someone could be in the house. Let's check it out."

A door slammed. Neighbors from across the street spilled out onto porches and the sidewalk to watch the drama unfolding.

A fourth car parked up the street. Not a patrol car. And an older man in a dark gray suit got out and joined them on the sidewalk.

"Hey, Chet." An officer approached him. "What are you doing here?"

"Heard the call. I was in the area. Got curious."

"We could use your help. Stay with the lady while we check out the house."

The man he called Chet stood by the car door, but his focus was the house.

The four officers drew their guns and two went inside, closing the front door behind them. One disappeared around the back of the house. The other stayed on the porch, beside the front door.

Tricia half expected her stalker to come bursting out. Then her attention shifted to the shadows surrounding her house. Bushes swished their branches in the wind. Shapes appeared, then disappeared. Ghostly fingers skimmed her spine, and she pulled her coat tighter around her. He could be watching and she had no idea who he was or why he was tormenting her.

Finally the officers came outside and searched the bushes in the front yard before disappearing around the house. Three officers emerged from the backyard a few minutes later. Officer Murray returned to the patrol car.

"We didn't find anyone. You can come inside." He waited for her to get out of the car, then escorted her through the front gate.

A surge of relief sped through her. She plodded up the steps to the front porch and into the house. The older man in the suit followed them as far as the foyer. Tricia dropped her purse and damp coat on a chair.

"No sign of forced entry," Officer Murray said. "Whoever did this had both keys or picked the locks."

Icy tentacles twisted around her heart. "The dead bolt was locked." She gulped in several breaths, trying to stay calm. "That means he had to have keys, right?"

"It's not safe for you to stay here until the locks are changed. Do you have somewhere to go? Friends? Family?"

"I'll figure something out."

"Someone will be here shortly to dust for finger prints. You can get the locks changed tomorrow."

They went into the living room. The older man hung back until motioned forward by Officer Murray.

"Chet, this is Tricia Landreth." He gestured toward the older man. "This is Chet Richardson, a detective who appears to be interested in your case." The detective nodded.

Her heart sped up. The detective had raised a brow at her name. She held her breath. Maybe he wouldn't make the connection with her uncle.

"What happened?" His tone of voice indicated this was a man who was all business.

She exhaled the breath she'd been holding.

"Go upstairs," the officer said. "The guy left a message in the bathroom."

After a glance at her, the detective walked up the stairs and quickly returned. He motioned for her to sit on the couch. "I am interested in this case."

Officer Murray retreated to the front door, but stayed on alert.

"I have some questions." The detective sat on the other end of the couch.

The detective's objective, direct approach helped her to think more clearly. She settled into the cushion on the couch and straightened her skirt.

"Start at the beginning and tell me what happened." He took out a notebook and pen.

She clasped her hands in front of her and repeated her story for him, then said, "At first I thought someone was playing a prank on me, or a former boyfriend was trying to send a message, but I don't date guys who smoke." She shivered and a wave of panic tightened her chest. She tamped it down.

"What does smoke have to do with it?"

"I smelled smoke when I got home tonight. I thought my cleaning service had sent a smoker. But the notes smelled of cigarette smoke too."

"I did smell smoke upstairs. Did you keep the letters?"

"They're in that top drawer." She pointed to a small desk along the inside wall.

"We'll take them with us when we leave." He surveyed the room. "You live alone?" His question sounded like an accusation. "Do you have a steady boyfriend?"

"Yes, I live alone. And I ended a relationship with Andy Pederson, a stock broker, about a week before the first letter arrived."

"Did he have keys to your house?"

"No. He didn't stay here."

"I'll check him out, along with other former boyfriends and anyone who appeared interested in you lately. I'll also check this MO with other agencies, in case he's done this before." The detective still spoke in a matter-of-fact tone.

"I may not be his first victim?" She concentrated on slow breathing, staying in control. This could be serious.

"It's possible." He hesitated, his dark eyes sharp and intelligent. "This guy went to a lot of trouble to get in here, most likely with copies of your keys. I'm assuming they're not easy to get."

Her mind raced. "I keep my keys in my purse, in a locked desk drawer when I'm at work. No one else has access to them."

"And the key to the drawer?" He wrote in the notebook, glanced up, wrote something else.

"In a small pouch I slip into my briefcase when I go to meetings."

"Could there be more than one key to the desk?"

She thought a moment. Then a sinking sensation settled inside her. "Maybe building maintenance keeps extra keys, in case someone loses theirs."

"Where do you work?"

"I'm a corporate lawyer with Talbot Enterprises, in the Talbot Building downtown."

"Lots of people. Lots of opportunities." He tapped his pen against his notebook. "Landreth? Any relation to Doug Landreth of Landreth Investigations?"

She hesitated long enough to spark a scowl from the detective. "He's my uncle." She grudgingly admitted it, though wished she could have avoided the truth.

"What did he say when you told him about this stalker?"

She squirmed under his scowling gaze. "I haven't told him."

"Why not?"

"I have my reasons." The whole situation was complicated, tied up in family dynamics and loyalties, involving her father. Nothing to do with Uncle Doug's crippled legs.

"He's a private investigator. A very good one. And he has excellent people working for him."

"I know."

"The police can investigate, but we can't provide protection for you. I've known your uncle for years. He can help you."

"I don't want his help." She was being irrational, but that's how she felt.

"Okay, let me spell this out for you. What if this guy happens to be a rapist or a killer? What if he's decided you're his next victim?" He punctuated his words with hand gestures. "When he grabs you, it'll be too late."

A knot tightened in her stomach. A physical pain deep down inside like nothing she'd ever experienced. She was in danger, her safety and security gone. "You're scaring me."

"I meant to."

CHAPTER 2

*N*ick Castellani slouched in the corner booth of the diner and sipped a cup of strong coffee. The diner opened early, served decent food, and wasn't far from his small house on the fringes of southwest Los Angeles. He'd gotten up at his usual time, though a long day with nothing to do stretched ahead of him. He'd rather be working.

The waitress set down his plate of hash browns, eggs, and toast, and topped off his coffee. Sally knew when he was in a bad mood. Knew why he was sitting there in jeans and T-shirt instead of his usual detective garb. His dark suit hung in his closet. He wouldn't be heading for the precinct today. Or any day soon.

He took a big bite of eggs and hash browns. And slathered jelly on a piece of toast. He chomped down on the toast and his cell phone rang.

He dragged his phone from his pocket and grimaced. Doug Landreth? Why the hell was he calling? He let the phone ring while he finished chewing the bite in his mouth.

Then he answered, out of curiosity. And habit.

"Hi, buddy. I realize I have no business asking you, but I need your help." Doug's tone was apologetic.

Nick took a sip of coffee. Buddy? He'd thought their friendship was dead and buried. Must be important. "Your timing is right. I'm on administrative leave."

"That's what I heard through my sources. What did you do this time?"

He'd failed his partner, but he wouldn't tell Doug that. "The lieutenant didn't like my explanation of how I saved myself and two others after my partner was killed. The investigation could last weeks."

Doug's half laugh came through the connection sounding strangled. "I'm not surprised. I worked with you long enough to know how you operate."

What was this conversation leading up to? Doug was acting like that mess five years ago didn't matter. Like it didn't matter they hadn't spoken in the four years since Doug had left L.A.

"We always did understand each other." Nick's words were tentative. "What do you want from me?"

"You to come to Portland. Today."

Nick sat up straight. "Why? What's up?"

"I have a temporary job for you. Tricia has a stalker."

Nick froze.

"He got into her house yesterday and left a death threat on her bathroom mirror."

Tricia. He hadn't seen her since the night their relationship abruptly ended. Ten years ago. He took another bite of hash browns and eggs. He hadn't forgotten a thing about her. Her soft skin under his fingertips. Her curled up beside him, touching, always touching. Her body beneath his, shattering.

He swallowed. "You want me to find this nut case?"

"No. Something more important. Tricia needs a full time bodyguard. My instincts tell me this guy is more than a stalker."

"She won't let me hang around as a bodyguard. She's your niece. Don't you have someone in your agency who can do the job?" Panic raised the timbre of his voice.

"One person is on vacation and the rest have cases they can't walk away from. Tricia refuses to leave town. I need someone 24/7. I can't leave her unprotected until this guy is caught."

Nick pushed his breakfast aside. And Doug couldn't do the job himself. That was the unspoken message. His legs were crippled from the car bomb that had killed his wife five years ago.

Intense physical therapy had gotten Doug back on his feet, but he walked with a cane. And endured the pain. That much Nick had learned from a mutual friend in Portland.

Nick's gut clenched into a tight knot. "I'm not the right person to be her bodyguard." Tricia would not want to see him again. What would her reaction be?

"She could be killed." A note of pleading in Doug's voice?

"Doug, I can't do it." He waved off Sally with the coffee pot.

"Swallow your pride and protect her."

"Pride isn't the problem." He did long to see her again, yet was afraid of his own feelings for her. She was the reason he'd stayed away from Portland, when he knew she'd moved back to town to take a job.

"That's part of it. The rest is your own bulldog way of getting things done. And that wrenching guilt you carry with you. That's why I want you on the job. You'll do whatever it takes to keep Tricia safe."

"It's that serious?"

"Chet Richardson is the detective on the case. He thinks the guy could be a serial killer. He's checking the MO with murders in other jurisdictions." His voice now had that distinctive authoritative air that was pure Doug.

"Chet's a good man. Dad used to talk about him when they worked together."

"He can't do anything except investigate. He can't keep her safe."

"And you think I can?" Had Doug changed his mind about him? He had to ask the question.

"Yes." An emphatic tone. "I trust you to protect her. And any insights you have about the stalker will help. You're a seasoned detective."

Nick hesitated. Took another sip of his rapidly cooling coffee.

"You owe me." Doug's words cut into the silence, challenging him.

Guilt wrenched Nick's gut. "Yes, I do." His mind flashed back to that awful night. He should have been there.

"I'm calling in all markers."

Tricia's life was at stake. Could he help Doug but keep his own feelings for Tricia out of it? A friend from college told him last year she'd never married, and had dumped other guys too. She was a single-minded career woman, independent as hell. But she was in danger.

He had no choice, no matter how difficult the assignment. He couldn't say no. He couldn't leave Tricia unprotected.

"I'll come." The most difficult words he'd uttered in a long time.

"I knew I could count on you to protect her." And the unspoken command. *With your life, if necessary.*

He'd do that for Doug. For Tricia.

Even from a thousand miles south, Nick could sense the smirk on Doug's face. "So, where's Tricia now?"

"At work. She spent the night in a hotel."

"What's the guy done so far?"

"He mailed two notes, then the break-in yesterday." He paused. "And a death threat scrawled on her bathroom mirror. Chet told me this morning that the only things missing, according to Tricia, are a red bra and matching panties. Trophies."

His gut clenched again. "Doesn't sound good. Could be a rapist who kills his victims."

"We do have one clue. He's most likely a heavy smoker. A lingering odor hung in the air when Tricia got home."

"Not much to go on. I'll book the first flight I can get and call you with my arrival time."

"I'll have a rental waiting for you." A short silence. "Thank you."

Could he work for Doug? Had enough time passed? The big question was whether Tricia would accept him as a bodyguard.

He had to try. "We've been through a lot together, it's the least I can do. I'll see you in a few hours." He ended the call.

Then he leaned against the cool Naugahyde of the booth. Thinking about Tricia. They had been evenly matched intellectually. The two years they dated, their focus had been getting through college and enjoying each other's company.

Until they graduated. Until their separate plans for the future tore them apart.

They'd had one hell of an argument the night they broke up. He'd keep her safe until the guy was caught. By honing his acting skills and keeping his distance, he'd come home with his heart intact.

～

TRICIA TURNED ONTO HER STREET, and the knots in her stomach tightened, until they were rock hard. The job she loved was in jeopardy. Something wasn't quite right with the financial details of the project she'd been assigned. She hadn't been able to make sense of the spreadsheet and her boss was blaming the delay on her. He'd sent her a scathing email this afternoon, telling her he'd fire her if she couldn't figure out the problem with the financing.

Evening darkness closed in as she arrived home and parked on her paved space to the right of the house. She'd bought an older house in an older neighborhood, without a garage. Which meant she had to enter the house through the front gate and front door or go around to the back door. Could buying this particular house have put her in more danger? She sat a moment, unwilling to leave the safety of her car.

He'd stolen her favorite red bra and panties.

The image of what he could be doing with her underwear had lingered all day. Crept into her consciousness, diverted her attention from her work.

She scanned the gate, the yard, the steps leading up to the porch. And the shadows on the porch. She shoved the car door open, and the pain in her stomach intensified. Holding the front door key between two fingers of her right hand, she glanced around again. She could stab someone with the key if she had to.

The wrought iron fence surrounding the front yard had been put up mainly for decoration, not to keep people out. She stopped in front of the gate. Dusk and the dark rain clouds created eerie shadows.

A car horn honked. She jumped, and grasped the gate to steady herself, then forced herself to take a deep breath. She was too jittery since the stalker targeted her. All she wanted was for her life to calm down, to return to normal.

She shuddered and peered into the shadows, searching again for anyone hiding next to the house.

The locks had been changed during the day, and the locksmith had delivered her new keys to her at work. She stared at the door of her house with a deep feeling of emptiness. Would she ever feel safe again?

A car door slammed.

She whirled around. A man walked toward her, his face in the shadows. She charged through the gate, and shoved it closed with a loud clang. And sprinted for the porch, her key ready to put in the lock.

"Tricia, wait. It's me, Nick."

She put the key in the door, turned it, then fumbled for the second key.

"Tricia, wait."

His voice. No, it couldn't be Nick. She didn't want it to be Nick. She unlocked the other lock and pushed the door open.

Then turned toward the gate, straining to see his features in the dim light.

Was he her stalker?

"Show yourself." Her voice shook with a combination of fear and anticipation.

He stepped into the muted light from the street lamp and her heart leapt into her throat, choking off any more words.

Standing on the sidewalk was a more mature version of the young man she'd dated and slept with while in college. The same dark brown hair waved back from his forehead. The same dark eyes drew her in.

Unbelievable. Nick was here. Mere feet away on the other

side of her gate. Excitement, accompanied by wariness, flared. She couldn't help but move down the steps, toward him.

"What are you doing here?" She found the words, her voice steadier this time. As she gazed at him, her pulse picked up. Tremors cascaded through her body.

Nick. The only man she'd ever wanted for her own.

He reached out and grasped a bar of the gate. "Waiting for you to come home." His words were quiet. His eyes focused on her face.

She stopped a few feet from the fence. "Why?" She clasped her briefcase and purse tighter, to still her shaking hands. What was wrong with her? Hadn't she learned anything? Men couldn't be trusted.

He laughed, but it sounded self-conscious. "Is that the way you greet an old friend?"

"Are we still friends?"

"I consider you a friend, Tricia." He drawled his words.

No. They couldn't be friends. There was nothing between them anymore. Besides, he was probably married. What's more, she didn't care. *Liar,* said the little voice inside that rarely lied.

"You haven't told me why you're here." She tried to sound calm, despite her inner turmoil.

"Doug sent me. He said you've had a stalker." His tone had become matter-of-fact, devoid of the friendly undertone. Like he'd flipped a switch.

"I knew that detective would call him, and Doug would interfere. Why did he send you? I thought you were a cop in L.A."

"I'm on temporary leave. Doug called me this morning and asked me to fly up. May I come in? Please." His smile was the same devilish smile that used to melt her insides.

He wasn't her stalker. Relief uncoiled in her midsection. But having him here sparked something else she didn't want to think about, setting her nerves on alert. She was afraid to let Nick into her home. She was afraid of her own buried feelings for him.

She gazed into the dark depths of his eyes, searching for the why. Though she hadn't seen him in a long time, she couldn't forget what he'd once meant to her. "Ah...I think you'd better go. I have a lot to do tonight."

"I want to check out the house, to make sure nothing else has happened."

"I assume Doug told you what I found last night."

He nodded.

"The locks were changed today. I'll be safe." She said the words but the web of fear in her body contradicted her.

"You're not going inside alone. No one has checked the house for you this evening, have they?"

"No." The apprehension returned, along with the rain that had threatened. The rain began lightly, increasing in intensity.

"He could have gotten in through a window." Nick's words challenged her. "You didn't check the windows."

"Of course I didn't. You saw me drive up and park." She pulled up the hood of her coat, her stomach clenching.

She made a decision. "Okay. You can come in. Long enough to look around. Then you're leaving." She emphasized the last words.

"Sit in your car while I search the house."

"I did that last night. I'm not doing it tonight. I'm going in with you."

"He could be inside, waiting for you to come home." He opened the gate and slipped through.

She headed for the porch. "I don't care. I'm going in. You can come too, if you want." She was being irrational, but she was tired of men telling her what to do.

"All right. We'll do it your way." His scowl added to the turmoil inside her, yet she also felt relief. She didn't have to face her house alone.

They walked up the steps and onto the porch with her very aware of the man next to her. He was well-built and muscular. That hadn't changed with the years, nor was it hidden by the jacket he wore. The scent of rain in the air mingled with the masculine, spicy scent of him she had always loved. Seeing him kindled memories of the great times they'd had together.

At the front door he halted her with a hand on her arm. He pushed the door all the way open. Then drew his gun from the shoulder holster under his jacket. He stepped inside, motioning her to follow him.

Once inside, she closed the door behind her, and turned the lock. She'd fasten the deadbolt after he left.

"Wait here." He held up a hand. "If you hear any noises, like a scuffle, get outside immediately and call 911."

"Okay."

He disappeared to the right, into the dining room, then the kitchen. She stood to the left of the door, clutching her brief-case and purse. Ready to run, listening for anything that sounded threatening.

He checked the downstairs, then crept upstairs. He was being thorough, but time crawled.

"All clear." He came down the stairs to the foyer. "No surprises." He shoved his gun into its holster.

"So, all I have hanging over my head is one death threat from last night." Her lame attempt to lighten the mood fell flat, even to her own ears.

"He's not going to get you, Tricia." His tone was completely serious.

She shuddered. "So, why did Uncle Doug send you? What does he expect you to do? Catch the guy?" She tried for calm detachment.

"I'm your new bodyguard."

White hot flashes of anger surged through her. "I don't want a bodyguard. If Doug hired you, I'm firing you. You're not hanging around here."

"Doug told me this morning that you'd refused to leave town or hide out while the police search for this guy."

"I can't leave town, leave my job. We're in the middle of a very important real estate acquisition that isn't going smoothly. I have to stay here and figure out why the deal is falling apart."

"Then I stay too, and keep you safe." The devilish smile crept back, accompanied by an exaggerated shrug. Captivating yet scary.

Uneasiness settled in. "I told you, you're fired."

"You didn't hire me. You can't fire me." His words challenged her. He moved closer.

Her heart rate accelerated and she backed up. "Leave now. I'm safe inside. You're not staying here, under any circumstances. Got that?"

First a stalker, now Nick. Totally different kinds of danger.

"I could sleep on your couch, in case the guy comes back." The words came out quietly, smoothly.

She recoiled at the thought. "No. Go away."

He stared at her for a moment. "Okay, I'll go, but not far. I got lucky and scored a parking space where I can see your house."

"You can't sleep in your car."

"I wasn't planning on sleeping."

"Leave. Go to your mother's. Doesn't she live in southeast Portland?"

He shook his head. "She lives in Virginia now, near my sister and her family. See you in the morning, Tricia." He went out the door, closing it behind him.

She rushed forward, checked the lower lock, flipped the dead bolt, and leaned against the cold oak. What just happened?

Nick.

CHAPTER 3

*N*ick's eyes snapped open. He gripped the steering wheel in front of him and pulled himself upright. Dark outside, not yet daylight. But he'd fallen asleep when he hadn't intended to.

Again.

He checked the time on his cell phone and groaned. He'd slept a whole hour. Guilt rushed through him, igniting flames of anger deep in his gut. Damn. No one would die because of him.

Again.

That was his vow. To himself. To Doug. To Tricia.

The guy could be anywhere, and they had no idea what he planned. Would he kidnap Tricia? Take her somewhere? Or invade her house and....

No...no... He shook his head to clear the images. He'd been a cop too long.

His gut seethed with anger and guilt as he wiped the condensation off the window with his sleeve.

Tricia was silhouetted in the light from her downstairs window. She was up and okay. His adrenalin rush slowly ebbed. He stretched his cramped muscles.

He hadn't failed her.

He'd keep Tricia safe, no matter what. He couldn't give Doug back his wife or the full use of his legs, but he could protect Tricia, despite her objections.

Tricia was even more gorgeous, more sensuous, than she'd been in college. He'd been drawn then to her exotic beauty. Maybe that's what attracted the killer. Her sensuality was provocative despite her attempts to tone it down with classic business clothes.

The steady light rain had finally stopped. He shivered and pulled his jacket tighter. In a few minutes she came out her front door, briefcase in hand, and walked down the steps, toward her gate.

He knew the instant she spotted him inside his car. She hesitated at the gate, obviously not wanting to face him. He waited. She squared her shoulders and raised her chin before opening the gate. He pushed the car door open and got out. "Good morning." With effort he kept his voice neutral.

"Good morning." She narrowed her eyes like she was trying to figure out how to get rid of him. "You slept out here last night?"

"I told you I was staying."

"Why?"

"You keep asking the same question. I'm your bodyguard. I'm not going to let that guy get to you." He grinned and tried to appear nonchalant.

"I fired you last night. I don't want anyone following me around."

"As I said last night, you didn't hire me, you can't fire me." He opened the passenger door of the SUV. "Get in. I'll drive you to work."

"Then I won't have my car downtown."

"I'll bring you home when you're ready."

"No. I'm driving myself."

He shook his head. "My orders are to stick with you on the way to work and heading home. And I'm going to go see Doug so I need my car."

She inhaled deeply, as if to give herself time to think. "No, Nick. This won't work."

He shrugged. "I don't see why not. I drive you and keep you safe and your uncle is happy, I'm happy, and you're happy."

"Why would having you around make me happy?" The edge in her voice was sharp enough to cut paper.

He stared at her. "Okay, not happy, but safe from the stalker. You do want to be safe, don't you?"

"Of course I do."

He gestured toward the open passenger door. "Please?" He could see her wavering. Then she got in the car and he shut the door. One short victory. Had she always been this difficult? Had he been blinded by his feelings for her?

"I'm going to call my uncle today and tell him you're fired." She greeted him with those words as he settled behind the wheel.

"I repeat, you can't fire me. I'm going to protect you, even from myself."

She gasped. "I'm not afraid of you."

"Well, I'm afraid of you, and the effect you have on me." The words escaped before he could stop them. At least that shut her up. But something else happened. He could see it in her eyes, a wariness that wasn't there before.

She didn't say anything, simply stared straight ahead while he drove through the traffic into downtown.

He pulled into a short term parking space on the street, a block from the office building where Tricia worked. And waited for a reaction.

"You could have let me out in front of the building," she said, right on cue. "You don't have to play guard dog. No one's going to kidnap me on a busy Portland street." The same sharp edge to her voice.

"Boss's orders. Besides, I'm going to check out security in the building, then go see Doug. I'll be back before you get off work." He got out and glanced up at the thick gray clouds overhead. At least it wasn't raining, so she couldn't accuse him of getting her wet.

She stepped out of the SUV and joined him on the sidewalk. "I may have to work late." They walked toward the Talbot Building.

"Doug is talking to your boss, to see if your hours can be more regular for a while, and see if it's possible for you to work at home at times."

She released an exasperated sigh. "Doug shouldn't interfere. It's my job, my responsibility. We're putting together a financial package for a large convention hotel for Portland."

"Better the deal jeopardized than your life." He sidestepped around an approaching couple. "Maybe you have a more understanding boss than you think you do."

She kept pace with him. "Hardly. I was assigned to Norm Talbot, the owner's son, for this project. Working with him is a challenge."

"Call my cell when you're about ready to leave the office. I'll be nearby, waiting for your call." He handed her a card with his number on it.

"I don't like depending on other people." She emphasized each word, then stuck the card in her purse.

"You're not taking the threat seriously. What if the guy came up to you, stuck a gun in your ribs, told you to keep quiet, keep walking?" The play of emotion on her face morphed into a glare.

"Won't happen." Her words were emphatic.

"It could." He grabbed her arm and reached his hand to her side, simulating a gun poking her in the ribs. "See how easily I touched you?"

"But we were walking together." The glare deepened and she pulled away.

"Maybe your stalker is someone you're frequently around. Someone who could get close to you. Remember, he had access to your keys." She exhaled, sounding frustrated. "Think about who you're in contact with. Tell me if anyone acts suspicious around you. Anyone watches you too closely. Anything out of the ordinary."

She pressed her lips together as if holding back another retort.

They reached the front door of the Talbot Building and Nick opened the outer door.

"I suppose you think you have to go inside."

"Yes, if I'm going to talk to security." Her heels clicked on the marble floor of the lobby as he followed her through the door.

"Morning, Ms. Landreth." The burly, gray-haired security guard greeted her with a smile. He stood next to a desk off to one side of the door.

"Good morning, Hal."

"Introduce me, please."

She mumbled something under her breath, then obliged. "This is Hal Roesch. He's worked security here for years." She turned to Hal. "This is Nick Castellani, who works for my uncle. He wants to talk to you."

"Right now?" Hal had a suspicious tone in his voice.

"I'll be back down."

"I can find my way to my office."

"But I can't unless you show me where it is."

Her eyes narrowed, but she led the way across the lobby to the elevator. Score one for him. She was at work and safe. He'd talk to the security guard and find out how safe.

THE ELEVATOR CLOSED ON NICK, blocking Tricia's view of him. What did he say earlier? *I'm afraid of you and the effect you have on me.*

What about the effect he had on *her*? She'd forgotten how much she simply enjoyed his company. He was easy to be with and she marveled at the way his mind puzzled out problems. And the way his smile warmed her heart.

Having him as a bodyguard wouldn't work. Surely if she reasoned with her uncle, she could convince him she didn't need Nick hanging around. She reached her office, picked up the phone, and punched in his number.

"I was waiting for you to call." She sensed his awareness of the situation in his words and in his tone. "How are you and Nick getting along?"

"Fantastic." She put as much sarcasm into one word as she could. "Call him off. I don't want him near me. I can't work with him around." She cringed. That didn't come out right.

"You can't work if you're dead." His tone was quiet, controlled. Typical Uncle Doug talk.

"You don't understand. The project I'm doing is important. I could lose my job if I don't figure out what is going wrong with the financing. I can't put my life on hold for weeks or months, until the guy is caught." Desperation tinged her words.

"Let me give you something else to consider. This morning Chet Richardson told me the FBI is investigating several deaths in other cities. They began with a stalker invading his victims' homes, leaving messages, and stealing underwear. He eventually kidnapped them, then raped and murdered them. Chet will know more after he talks to the profiler."

Tricia clutched the phone and shivered. That icy chill returned, the same chill as when she'd seen the scrawled message. This couldn't be happening. "But I have to keep working." She tried for a convincing tone.

"Then you have to have a bodyguard. The guy broke into your house and left a death threat. Your life is at stake." He paused. "Think about that today."

"I don't have time to think about it. I have work to do."

"I know you don't want my help, but I can't sit back and not do everything I can to protect you. You're my niece. Family." He paused. "That's why I called Nick."

"Um...I'll talk to you later." She stared at the phone, then dropped it into its cradle. So much for convincing her uncle to send Nick back to Los Angeles. Why did it have to be Nick?

NICK SPENT five minutes by the information desk in the lobby. Observing. The unarmed security guard relaxed in his chair, seemingly unconcerned about anything except passing the time. Despite being the lone man watching the front door and the people coming in and out, he only glanced twice toward the door. Spoke to no one. Questioned no one.

Anger roiled inside Nick. He stayed where he was for a few more minutes, to get his anger under control, then crossed the lobby. He wanted information, not confrontation. He wanted to know how close he'd have to stay to Tricia, to protect her.

He decided on a direct approach. "Hi. I have a question. What other security measures do you have in this building, besides you stationed at the front door?" He kept his expression nonchalant and his hands where Hal could see them.

"Why? Is something wrong?" Hal jumped up to face Nick, a scowling frown in place.

Nick scrapped that approach. "I see you have the front door covered. What backup do you have?"

Hal studied Nick. "Why are you asking?" His words were deliberate and forceful.

Okay, he wasn't the talkative kind. How much to tell him was the problem. Nick hadn't discussed it with Doug. "I'd like to know what security measures are in effect in this building, how the employees are being protected."

"We have a surveillance system, lots of cameras. We take care of security." His voice was gruff and decisive. Maybe Nick underestimated the guy. He glanced around the lobby and spotted two surveillance cameras.

"Are the cameras monitored? Are the videos viewed regularly? How does the system work?"

"That's privileged information. If anything happens, we call the police. We don't want anyone snooping around."

The stubborn lift of Hal's jaw told Nick he wouldn't get the information he wanted from this man. "Sorry I bothered you." He headed for the door. Maybe Doug would have better luck. Nick's instincts told him security here was too lax to do Tricia any good if the stalker worked in this building. Every day she spent here put her in danger.

CHAPTER 4

$\mathcal{N}$ick parked in front of Doug's detective agency, under an elm tree that had lost about half its golden leaves of fall. Their first meeting yesterday had been cordial, but strained. A prickle of anticipation quickened Nick's pulse and sweat formed on his brow despite the cool, cloudy morning.

He laughed at himself. Kind of ironic that a different kind of assignment miles from his job and normal responsibilities had him on edge. He had a suspicion his whole future hinged on what would happen here in Portland. He tried to shrug off the feeling. He was here to do a temporary job. For Doug. That's all.

Nick had worked in the Gang and Narcotics Division with Doug down in L.A., before Doug's legs were injured. A quick stab of guilt hit his gut. For now, he'd focus on what had been right in their relationship and how nice to be working together again. Too bad the reason was Tricia.

He went inside the one-story brick-faced building.

"Doug's in his office." Meagan smiled at him. He'd met the

competent receptionist yesterday and had immediately sensed her importance to the agency.

Meagan came from behind her desk. "Tell Doug I'm coming with coffee. Fresh pot brewing. Do you want yours black?"

"Yes, thanks." He sauntered down the hall and into Doug's office at the far corner of the building.

Doug glanced up with his signature smirk, half smile, half grimace. He didn't look any different than he had four years ago. The same dark brown hair. The same lean build. The same deep penetrating dark eyes. Then the similarity ended.

No more dark suit, the usual detective uniform. No more clean-shaven face. The five o'clock shadow suited him. A leather jacket hung on a coat rack in the corner. His muscular upper body was encased in a snug pullover shirt. As long as he was sitting, you couldn't tell his legs were crippled.

Doug rose to greet him, his limp obvious as he came out from behind his desk and grasped Nick's hand. "I'm glad you're here. I was serious when I said I need your help."

Nick mumbled a greeting. "All we have to do is keep Tricia safe until the guy is caught." He dropped into the chair in front of the desk. "Meagan said to tell you fresh coffee is coming."

Doug sank into his own chair, silhouetted by the window.

Light streamed through the one window and bounced off the glass-covered prints on the wall. Views of Mt. Hood and the Columbia River. The pictures made Nick feel more at home.

Meagan appeared at the door, coffee pot in hand, and carrying one cup. She set the cup for Nick on the front edge of Doug's desk and filled it. Then filled Doug's empty cup.

"Thanks," Doug said. She left quickly.

Nick chuckled. "Some things never change." He lifted his cup in a salute and took a sip.

"Yes, I won't give up my caffeine addiction." Doug's smirk

flashed, then his expression turned serious. "I'm counting on you to protect Tricia." His deep penetrating gaze carried its own challenge. "But I could also use help with something else." The words sounded ominous, delivered in a worried tone.

"Something more important than protecting Tricia?"

"No." He shook his head. "Merely information. You're on the streets of L.A. You see what's going on." He picked up his coffee cup and took a sip.

"Are you asking if I know where Moreno is?" He should have guessed.

"Do you?"

"Not exactly. But he's been back in Los Angeles for almost a year."

"That's what I heard. Are you positive it's the same guy? Ramon Moreno?" He swiveled to his computer and with a couple of clicks, pulled up a picture.

Nick studied the image. "That's him. The newspapers have identified him by his full name, including his mother's surname. Ramon Jesus Moreno Herrera."

"What about his organization?" Doug swiveled back to the desk.

Nick gestured with his hands. "Bigger and more dangerous than ever. We did stop one of his cash payments last month. $13 million heading to Mexico in a false-bottomed truck. Payment for a meth delivery."

"Impressive. How did you find out about that?"

"We have a guy working the streets for information. Eddie Velasquez."

"Velasquez? That drug-addicted weasel? He's a dealer. Scum."

"A double-dealer now."

"Why? What made him switch sides?"

"Remember Camille? His young sister who tried to help him and tried to help us?"

"Yeah. She was a pretty little thing."

"Not any more. Moreno brought his oldest son, Armando, with him when he came back from Mexico. Since you killed his two younger sons who were trying to protect that heroin shipment. Armando got to Camille, hooked her on meth, got her pregnant, then killed her."

"Revenge?" His tone was deep, steely. "He lost a $20 million shipment of Colombian heroin and $5 million in cash that night, along with his sons. Could he be targeting the people I knew down there?"

"That's one theory. Since he wasn't able to kill you with that car bomb. Just Patti."

"Someone thought of the revenge theory?"

"The captain himself." Nick took a sip of his cooling coffee. Then finished off the cup.

"And you trust Velasquez?"

"He's on our side. And clean."

"How many more people are going to die before Moreno's satisfied?"

"You're at the top of his list. You may not be so lucky next time." Nick's gut clenched. The car bomb had left Doug close to death.

"He'll have to come here. I'm not going to L.A. to make it easy for him."

"He may do that. He's in solid with the Sinaloa cartel. There's talk he plans to expand his drug empire into the northwest, with the narcos' blessing."

A frown creased Doug's brow. "Why is Moreno coming up here? Why not Chicago or the east coast?"

"He hates unfinished business. Eliminating you is part of his plan, but only part. Building a strong northwest drug business is the ultimate goal. He has access to quality heroin, meth, and cocaine through the cartel. And a pipeline up the west coast."

Doug swiveled his chair so he could see out the window. "I came to Portland to open my agency for a reason, besides being close to my mother as she gets older. I came to escape the drug gangs in L.A. Escape the drugs themselves and what they do to people."

"So what's your agency focus? I assume it's not providing bodyguard services."

"No, it isn't. Unless it's a woman hiding from an abusive spouse. We've taken those cases. Mostly we focus on insurance fraud, finding lost kids, helping lawyers with investigations. Whatever needs doing that isn't of a violent nature." He spun away from the window, a deep scowl on his face. "And now Moreno is going to bring his drugs and his violence to me."

"I'm afraid so. He plans to consolidate the drug business here."

"I'll contact Alison Steele and tell her to steer clear of L.A. She's on vacation and was going to visit her old neighborhood, to see friends."

"Might not be safe for her if Moreno's hoods connect her to you."

"She should come home anyway. Alison is one of the best. She could help with Tricia's stalker."

"Good." Nick hesitated. "From the information I have so far, I'm thinking her stalker is crafty and intelligent, works in that building, and has access to Tricia."

"You haven't been here long enough to have that kind of information." Doug's tone underscored his disbelief.

"Maybe. But I don't have confidence in the security in the building. Someone got to her keys."

"That's speculation too." Doug leaned back in his chair, coffee cup in his hand. "Chet's waiting for the report on the locks, to see if they show signs they were picked. An expert is taking them apart."

"The guy locked the dead bolt when he left the house."

"He could have found another way out of the house."

"But the evidence doesn't point that way." Nick forced a laugh. "You never did trust my assumptions based on facts."

"There's times when I should have." Pain flashed in Doug's eyes.

Silence dangled in the air between them. What could he possibly say that would help? A zap of guilt hit his gut. He hadn't been there that evening. Because he'd fallen asleep out of pure exhaustion.

Doug took a big breath, as if he were flushing out that pain. Then he leaned forward, the moment gone. "We may never know how the guy got into Tricia's house. But, you're concerned about security at the office, in case he works in the same building as Tricia."

Nick pushed aside thoughts of L.A. The priority was the stalker targeting Tricia. The past could wait. But he also had a premonition that the past would fester under the surface and break through later. Then they'd have to deal with the long-standing issues between them.

"Yep. It's an older building with plenty of places someone could hide." Nick shrugged. "The security guard in the lobby admitted there are surveillance cameras but wouldn't tell me if they're monitored or if the videos are viewed when necessary."

"If Chet has time, I'll see if he can check out the security. The police can get cooperation when we can't. Chet will tell me what information he can that will help us protect her." He pushed a business card across the desk. "Call him if you find out anything. Your role is strictly bodyguard."

Nick picked up the card and put it in his wallet. "Understood. That's a relief that the police here are willing to share information." He was familiar with the system from the police side. Not the PI side. He was more comfortable being a cop.

Doug leaned forward, his gaze intense. "Why is Tricia so determined that you shouldn't be her bodyguard?"

The question wasn't unexpected. "She called, I take it."

Doug nodded. "Why?" That one word carried immense power.

Nick hesitated, gathering his thoughts. "Possibly two reasons. She's uncomfortable being around me because of our earlier relationship. Or, she could be reacting as she would to anyone who gets in her space. She's very independent. She says the project she's working on is important and her boss seems to be making demands." He shook his head. "I don't have a good answer."

"Yeah, you're right about Tricia being independent," Doug said. "And she's as stubborn as they come. More like her father than she's willing to admit."

"So your brother, Adam, was stubborn and independent too?"

"He couldn't handle marriage and the responsibilities of raising a daughter."

"She told me she was real young when he left for good."

Doug nodded. "He did send money. But couldn't bother to come himself, once his mistress agreed to go to Vegas with him."

"That must of hurt Tricia as well as her mother."

"It did." Doug narrowed his eyes. "Is there still something between you two that could interfere with protecting her?"

"We haven't had any contact in ten years. So, no."

"Did you have a huge argument when you broke up? Is there an unresolved problem between you?"

"Yeah, we had an argument the last night. I made a tactical mistake. I took the rookie job in L.A. and then asked her to go with me. That's when she broadsided me with the news she had a full-ride scholarship to law school in New York and had accepted it. She left for New York. I left for L.A. We were both angry."

"You hadn't been talking? You hadn't been making plans for the future?"

"I told her I'd contacted you about a job down there."

Doug chuckled. And added that all-knowing look that told Nick he was a chump for making assumptions. "And now you're starting over. Maybe you can become simply friends."

"That's my intention. She has issues."

"So do you. Don't do anything stupid while you're here."

"Like fall for Tricia again? Won't happen. She was shocked when I showed up at her house unannounced. She wasn't happy to see me."

"So I gathered."

"Do you regret bringing me up here?"

Doug grimaced, hesitated a second. "No...no. I trust you. You're the best man for the job. As long as your feelings for Tricia don't get in the way."

He stared at Nick for what seemed like a long time. Nick sensed his ambivalence. Then Doug pulled a key from his drawer and put it on the desk. "Here's a key to my house. You can shower and crash there in the spare bedroom, if Tricia keeps you locked out."

"Thanks. And I won't let anything interfere." Nick picked up the key. And hoped he could keep the promise.

~

TRICIA'S STOMACH CHURNED. She collapsed against the back of her desk chair. The total on the spreadsheet couldn't be correct. She squinted at the numbers on the monitor in front of her. Yesterday morning the financial spreadsheet had balanced. This afternoon something was wrong with the figures.

She pushed her chair away from the desk. Something, or someone, had altered the calculations. She got up and paced the floor of her small office. No wonder Talbot was angry. He'd seen the incorrect numbers. He'd figured out that the spreadsheet was wrong.

He'd threatened to fire her in that email yesterday afternoon. He expected her to fix the problem, whatever it was. At least he hadn't said anything about firing her at the evening meeting. He hadn't wanted her assigned to the hotel project. His own ego problem. She'd been with the company longer than Norm Talbot, and he was the owner's son.

Was he trying to get rid of her while his father was in Europe on a honeymoon with his new wife? Getting fired would hurt her professional reputation when she looked for another job.

She couldn't let that happen. She'd loved her job, up until two weeks ago, when she'd been thrust into the middle of the hotel project by CEO Jerome Talbot. He trusted her judgment. But she wasn't getting cooperation from other members of the project team.

She returned to her chair and scooted to the desk. Then clicked through the pages searching for what could be missing from the file on the server. If someone changed the file, she should have been notified immediately. Surely whoever made changes knew she'd have questions. She was the lawyer vetting the project. She was the one with the responsibility to judge the entire project as feasible or not. She was the one who should always have the up-to-date information. Yet something was missing.

Why?

She scowled at the monitor and mentally reviewed the list of investors. A group of ten. Then she counted the names on the spreadsheet. Nine.

She read through the list out loud. The Stevenson name was missing. She remembered seeing his name last month when the preliminary figures came through, before she was assigned specifically to the project. She'd met the man a couple of years earlier when he was involved in another real estate acquisition with Talbot Enterprises. She'd bargained with his lawyers. He was an astute businessman.

Was the missing name an oversight? Or did Stevenson pull out of the deal? She wanted answers.

She picked up the phone and punched in the number for the finance department. "Becky, I'd like to speak to Mr. Parker. It's important."

Becky put her on hold. Tricia tapped her finger tips on the phone. And waited.

"I'm sorry, Mr. Parker isn't available."

"Ask him when I can talk to him."

"Not today." The answer came too quickly. Tricia stiffened. "Tell him the Stevenson bid is missing from the project file on the server. I need a copy. Immediately."

"I'll tell him, when he's available." The line went dead. Becky hung up on her.

Tricia put down the phone. She'd had reservations about this hotel project from the very beginning. Too ambitious. Too many rooms for a city the size of Portland. They would have to attract the very large conventions to fill the rooms. She wasn't sure Portland had enough attractions to pull in those convention goers.

Then, several days before he left town, the elder Talbot had assigned her directly to the project, over the objections of his son, the project manager. For two weeks the younger Talbot and the finance department had blocked her attempts to do her job. The job of making sure this project was feasible.

If only Jane hadn't retired. Tricia would have been able to call on her for the information she needed. Was there someone else in the finance department she could trust?

Delays in this project had come from the finance department, which was why the elder Talbot had wanted her legal oversight. As far as the missing bid, the possibilities were a cover up or a simple mistake. Her intuition told her something was wrong. Her bet was a cover up. And Norm Talbot blamed her. Why?

She scrolled through the file and rechecked the figures. Though she was almost positive she wouldn't get a different total, she had to try one more time.

She was retracing the pages of the project from the beginning when there was a knock on the door. Then the door opened.

"The document you wanted is in here." A clerk came in and handed Tricia a manila folder at least three inches thick. "These are hard copies of the paperwork. Mr. Parker wants the file in his office by 5:00. Bring it to the receptionist."

She left quickly, closing the door behind her. Tricia glanced at the clock on the wall. Two hours to review this massive file. Busy work. To keep her from asking more questions.

Another stalling tactic to keep her from the facts. She picked up the top page. Chronological order. Okay, that helped. She began sorting the stack of papers. Was the bid withdrawn? What weren't they telling her?

Randolph Parker had been hired three years ago as Chief Financial Officer. Was he setting her up to take the blame for something he did? Maybe the answer was in this massive file.

She grabbed her laptop from her briefcase and hooked it up to the scanner in her office. Then she opened the scanner and picked up the top sheet of paper. She'd scan the most important documents into a file on her laptop, then she'd have them at home with her. Somehow she'd figure out what was going on. Then challenge Parker when she had enough evidence.

CHAPTER 5

"This is ridiculous. I don't need a bodyguard." Tricia frowned at Nick, and attempted an intimidating glare. He was leaning against the marble pillar in the foyer of the office building, his captivating good looks defying her to ignore him as a man. He had the dark Mediterranean complexion and hot appeal he'd inherited from his Italian father. Damn. He belonged in L.A., far from her.

She belonged in Portland, far from him. Was she afraid to be near him? The last thing she needed was to get involved with him again.

"Sorry. Doug is the expert. He believes the kind of protection you need requires a bodyguard." His statement was devoid of feeling as if she were another job to him.

That bothered her. Despite what had happened between them, she'd never found a man who appealed to her like he did. She cringed. *Don't go there.*

Nick reached for her briefcase, and she jerked it away. "I can carry it." She warned him off with another glare she hoped didn't show her panic.

"I'm only trying to help." Nick's lopsided grin revived too many memories, the kind she'd tried to erase but hadn't succeeded.

They went through the front door and out onto the street, into the fall evening. At least there was no rain tonight.

"Let's have dinner at the grill on Tenth. I'm craving a good steak." Nick headed down the sidewalk, to the left. "And it's neutral territory for our first discussion."

"We've nothing to discuss. Take me home, drop me off, then do whatever you want. I'm taking work home tonight. I'm going to be very busy."

"I'm not leaving you alone." He moved closer and his voice escalated in tone. "There's a guy out there who wants to kill you and do other things to you first. Don't you get it?"

She tried to shush him with a shake of her head and a wave of her hand, before someone else heard him.

"Tricia, you have no choice. You need protection. Unless you want to find out what this guy has in mind." He scowled, his dark brows knitting together. "I guarantee you won't like it."

"You're trying to scare me." Her shoulders and arms began shaking, as much from the ferocity of his words as from the vivid picture he painted. He was right. Damn, he was right.

But he wasn't coming inside her house. He could sleep in his car if he wanted to. She didn't care. Having him near brought back too many memories of falling asleep in his arms, their passion spent.

She had kept telling herself back then that she didn't want a deeper relationship. Just the great sex. She'd had plans that didn't include him. And he'd had plans that wouldn't work for her. That job in L.A. Yet she'd wanted more from him, but was too scared to try to work things out.

And she was still scared. The past ten years seemed to have melted away. They were together and the old feelings between them were returning. She felt it. She saw it in his eyes and his smile.

He continued walking toward the restaurant and she gave in. She'd worked through lunch and snacked from the machines in the afternoon and was hungry. "Okay, dinner. Nothing more."

He flashed her a look she couldn't decipher, then gripped her elbow and steered her through the quitting-time crowd, to the restaurant.

The hostess showed them to a familiar table for two next to a mahogany panel that separated the dining room from the bar. They had sat at this very table when they'd come here early in their relationship. Tricia would have requested a different table, but one glance at the devilish spark in Nick's eyes told her he'd know exactly why she wanted the change.

Nick directed her to take the chair with her back to the front windows. Undoubtedly so he'd see whoever came through the door. She settled into the mahogany chair and lifted the napkin off the white tablecloth and placed it in her lap. The hostess handed them the menus then departed. A server appeared with two water glasses.

Tricia ignored the menu. She knew what she wanted. This was one of her favorite restaurants, though she usually avoided sitting at this table. As students on budgets, they hadn't been able to eat here more than a few times. Now she could afford eating here when she wanted. She liked the rich mahogany pillars and panels and the dim lighting of the interior. The atmosphere seemed to calm her after a hectic day of work.

After they ordered, Nick took a sip of water, then stared at her. She couldn't decide how to interpret the stare. His focus seemed miles away, in another dimension. This was not the same man she'd dated in college. He'd changed. But so had she.

His lips quirked into a half smile. "This restaurant played a part in our lives back in college. It's where we celebrated."

"Let's forget the past."

"I'll never forget." His words took on an intimate tone.

A mild panic built inside her. "You didn't come here to reminisce."

"Okay, change of subject." Nick's tone switched to brusque. "Tell me what happened, from the beginning. Doug told me, but I want to hear the story from you."

Her chest constricted. All the nerve endings in her body tightened. She didn't want to think about that night. But Nick was trying to help. Reluctantly she related the story of the letters and the message on the mirror. When she'd finished, she looked down at her napkin, to collect herself. After a few deep breaths, the tightness in her body eased.

Nick's intense scrutiny rattled her.

"Not much to work with." His words were quiet. "He's playing mind games with you. He must realize the police are involved. He may not know you have an uncle who runs a detective agency. The guy may be smart, but you have a lot of smart people on your side."

"Why did he pick me?"

"When we figure that out, we'll know who he is. In the meantime, Chet Richardson is waiting for more information from the FBI."

"Doug told me that the detective thinks it could be a serial killer." The tightness in her chest returned.

"One possibility. If there are similar crimes out there, he'll find out. In the meantime, my primary concern is keeping you safe, despite you not wanting me around."

How could she argue against his logic? If she didn't let him protect her, then whatever happened would be her fault. "I don't like the idea of a bodyguard." He might protect her from the stalker, but she'd have to keep her heart safe from him.

"I repeat. You have no choice." His dark eyes bore into hers. "I'm not leaving. I'm not going to make it easy for this maniac. The thought of who he is and what he plans to do to you churns up my insides. I'm sure it's affecting you too."

"Yes." Except what she felt was a deep chill to go along with the ever present fear. She was determined to keep working to unravel the mess the hotel project had become. Nick and Doug and the police could handle the investigation. Though she did admit, at least to herself, the threat was serious.

The clink of glasses and silverware on plates echoed in the room. The evening crowd had descended and the restaurant quickly filled. The server appeared with their order.

She took a bite of her seafood fettuccine, then put her fork down. The dish didn't taste as good as it usually did. Was it because Nick sat across the table from her, calmly stabbing a bite of steak, while her stomach did strange flip flops? They hadn't shared a meal in years. Yet it felt right in a strange way. *I can't fall for Nicolas Castellani again.*

She had to get through the rest of this dinner and get safely home.

Without Nick.

She couldn't risk the temptation of having him in her house.

"Do you have a current boyfriend?"

The question startled her, though it shouldn't have. Any bodyguard would have asked. But coming from Nick, the question held more meaning.

He took another bite of steak, his expression bland.

She didn't want to answer, because she'd have to admit she'd dumped another guy who got too close.

"You're stalling." His dark eyes challenged her.

She frowned and speared a bite of shrimp. "I broke up with Andy Pederson about a week before the first letter. But it's not him retaliating." She added the last bit quickly, before he could say anything. She put the shrimp into her mouth and chewed while thinking of his question in more depth.

"And you're positive? Were you engaged or simply dating?"

"I'm positive. It's not his style. For a while we had fun, then he started getting serious and talking marriage. I suspected a proposal was coming, so I told him I wasn't interested in long term. He didn't take the rejection well."

Nick flinched, verifying that he hadn't taken their breakup well, either. She hadn't heard from him since that long ago night. Until he showed up at her house yesterday evening.

"So who else is on the dumped list who could be upset?" His subdued tone indicated he was thinking about the past too.

"I don't usually date a guy long enough for him to get ideas." She raised her chin. "I've learned a few lessons over the years."

"Why was Andy different?"

"He's a stock broker and talked about going to Wall Street. He has big plans for his future and I had no idea they included me, since I made sure I told him I'm happy with my job and intend to stay in Portland. He figured I'd change my mind. A big ego to go with his bank account."

"He expected you to go with him?"

"He thought I'd be happy to quit my job, sell my house, and go with him to New York, when he gets his dream job. He's waiting for the right break." She held her breath, expecting Nick to accuse her of not wanting to go to L.A. with him.

"So, probably not Andy," Nick said.

She released the breath. He was focused on the stalker.

"The police will check out the guys you've dated lately and anyone who's been interested in you in any way. Stalkers have a curious MO and don't always know what they want when they begin. The guy could be someone who's familiar to you, or a serial killer who's come to town searching for his next victim. Or both."

Her throat constricted. "It could be anyone." The words barely squeaked out.

"That's the reason Doug called me. You can't be alone until he's caught."

She glanced around the crowded room. "He could be anywhere, even in this room."

"That's right. Some women get away from their attackers and some don't." His face twisted into a grimace.

"You're thinking about your experiences as a cop."

"Yes. Not all stalkers and rapists let their victims live. He could be an unpredictable psychopath."

That chill slid down her backbone again. "And you think this guy is planning rape and murder?"

"That's what the message implies." His tone was emphatic.

Being without protection was stupid. But Nick was a danger in his own way. A war raged inside her. Her precious independence versus protection from a potential killer. She gazed at Nick for a long time, her emotions a tangled mess.

Finally, she sighed. "Okay, he's broken into my home. Do you think he'll try to kidnap me?"

"Yes." The same emphatic tone.

A knot tightened in her stomach. "You're scaring me again."

"Good. I don't want you to think this will end on its own.

He's going to escalate. Maybe quickly, maybe slowly. You could be a target for some kind of rage directed at women in general."

She forked a bite of scallop, despite her disappearing appetite. "You're not going to use me as bait."

"Oh, no. My goal, and Doug's, is protecting you. We'll let the police catch him. For certain guys the anticipation and the fantasies are a bigger part of the process than the actual rape and murder. Remember your red underwear."

"I can't forget." Not even when focused on her work.

"Dragging things out gives the pervert a strange sense of power and control. A serial rapist who's going from victim to victim is the most dangerous kind. Especially if he's intelligent and has a plan. We'll try to mess with those plans."

Her heart clenched. "Okay, I get it. You're telling me this for my own good, so I won't get careless. This guy's dangerous."

"There's no predicting what he'll do once he has you." He grimaced. "Which is why he's not getting his hands on you. And why I'm here to protect you."

She stared at him, at the determination in his gaze, feeling safer than she had since the stalker sent the first letter. "So, what happens now?"

"I take you home and stay with you. I've slept on a lot of couches, but I won't sleep much, until he's caught."

She hesitated.

"What would convince you? Getting grabbed off the street?" His words stung.

"No." She shook her head. "I have a guest room. You won't have to sleep on my couch."

A small smile. "I appreciate a bed. I don't sleep good on couches."

Nick in the next room? She had no choice if she wanted to

remain in Portland and continue working. She wasn't stupid. Staying alone was dangerous. If anyone could help her, it was Nick. But she couldn't fall in love with him. *Catch the guy, then go away*, she wanted to shout at him. *I don't dare love you.*

CHAPTER 6

*O*f course she'd objected when he locked her inside the SUV and told her to stay there while he checked out the house. He'd parked behind her car, next to the front yard fence, then glanced at the dark shadows surrounding the house. Someone could have broken into the house while they were gone.

He hadn't given in to her arguments, but took her keys and went inside. And didn't find anything out of place.

He returned to the vehicle and opened her door, offering his hand to help her out.

"I can get out of a car." She brushed his hand aside. "I stayed out here for nothing. You aren't going to do this every day, are you?" Her sharp words hit him in a vulnerable spot.

"If I have to." He thought he'd scared her enough. Obviously not. His job was to keep her safe. And keep his hands off her, though being close to her kept his body humming and made his job more difficult.

Nothing in his life had been easy. Why should things change?

He bit back another retort and opened the rear of the SUV. He took out his suitcase, his briefcase, and the two plastic shopping bags of extra clothes and toiletries he'd bought. He had a feeling he'd be around here for a while and he'd need more than he'd packed in a hurry to make his flight.

A brisk breeze whipped Tricia's long brown hair into her face. The wind stirred the leaves on the ground and the branches of trees and bushes. He followed her through the gate and up the steps to the porch in silence. An uncomfortable silence. He was playing a waiting game. Waiting for her to realize the full extent of the danger. Waiting for the guy to be caught. Waiting until he could return to L.A. and his job. Let her have her moods, as long as he could stay with her and protect her from that creep.

Once inside the house, he set his suitcase and plastic bags on the floor, then shut and locked the door. He flipped the dead bolt, then put her keys in his pocket.

She glared at him. "You took my keys."

"If they're in my pocket, no one at the office can take them out of your purse."

"So you're the keeper of the keys." She scowled and pursed her lips. "This won't work." She headed for the living room.

She didn't want him in her space. But why? Did she believe she could take care of herself? Or, she didn't want him to be the one taking care of her? An interesting question. Not one he'd risk asking.

They wouldn't be sleeping together. He was here for her safety. Nothing else. Yeah. Tell that to his libido.

Yet he saw something in her gaze that told him she wasn't as immune to him as she wanted him to think. There was a subtle heat there, deep down in the depths of those vivid brown eyes. Maybe a longing for what might have been? Her prim no-nonsense business suit clung to her curves. She couldn't help that she was one sensuous woman. And he should think about something other than the way their bodies had fit together.

She was staring up the stairs.

"There's nothing up there. I searched everywhere."

She nodded. "I know. Simply nerves." She put one foot on the bottom stair.

"Do you want me to walk up with you?"

She shook her head. "No. I'm going to change my clothes. I'll be right down." She tromped up the stairs, challenging each step decisively. No hesitation once she'd made up her mind. She'd get through this. She had spunk and courage, traits he'd always admired in her.

He set his briefcase on the couch, and glanced around the living room. He hadn't paid too much attention the night before. Immediately he could tell the house belonged to her. Even the scent in the air reeked of her feminine perfume, a faint woodsy fragrance. Not a sweet flowery scent for an exotic beauty like Tricia.

A beige leather couch separated the living room from the hallway, with red and yellow pillows adding splashes of color. Two other chairs of beige leather had accent pillows of forest green and a lighter green. The artwork on the walls consisted of prints and a couple of water colors, with one oil painting of a fall forest in shades of orange and gold over the mantel. A combination that blended well.

He crossed to the bookcase and examined the spines. Books on history, design, and a mix of fiction types, including romance and thrillers. A stereo and racks of CDs. Classical, easy listening, jazz. Interesting assortment, yet pure Tricia.

No newspapers, magazines, discarded junk mail. Her television hid behind the doors of a cabinet. Nothing out of place.

This house wasn't like the bland apartment she and her two roommates had shared while in college. His apartment had been equally bland. He'd lived alone so was able to have her over for an occasional night. He recalled trying to get her to move in with him and her immediate withdrawing for a while. A subtle warning he hadn't heeded.

She came down the stairs. "I'm sorry. I could have showed you to the guest room. First door on the left, top of the stairs."

He took his suitcase and shopping bags up the stairs and into the sparsely furnished room. When he returned downstairs, he opened his briefcase, with his laptop and files, and sat on one end of the beige leather couch.

Tricia took the other end. She wore slacks and a sweater that said career woman, don't mess with me. He got the message.

He set his laptop on the coffee table in front of them and several folders on the couch between them. A slight barrier, but better than none. So far her attitude toward him had fluctuated between hostile and neutral. He'd stay behind the walls he erected to keep her out. Hell, he had to keep his hands off her somehow. *Take it day by day. You can do this.*

TRICIA SET her laptop on the coffee table and booted the machine. While the software loaded, she dug into her briefcase and found the file with the notes she'd written earlier, when she'd discovered the problem with the totals. With any luck, she'd locate the information she needed tonight on those pages she'd scanned to her computer. Then she could go to Talbot with facts instead of speculation.

If Nick wasn't too much of a distraction.

You could go down the hall to your small office. Her rational mind presented her with the possibility. Yet a part of her didn't want to leave Nick in the living room by himself. She liked his company. And he was trying to help her.

Besides, she was more comfortable out here on the couch. He sat to her right, within her peripheral vision. For a better view, she turned her head slightly. Then focused on her laptop, to shut him out. She'd spent years trying to forget him.

"Wireless?"

"Uh, yes." She recited the password slowly, while he punched it in. Then she located the file with the scanned documents.

"An email from Doug." Nick read it to her. "No new information. No forced entry. The guy had copies of Tricia's keys, or picked the locks." He glanced at her. "That's what Chet Richardson said."

"I never left my keys out where anyone could borrow them, even for a few minutes." Her tone was defensive, but she couldn't help it. She opened the file on her laptop and scrolled through the pages.

"No one is accusing you of anything. We're checking the facts that we know."

"I didn't ask for this problem. I have work to do."

"So what are you working on that's so important you can't leave town for your own safety?"

"It's a privately-financed luxury convention hotel for Portland. Bringing in the big conventions would help local businesses." She scowled at him. "These disruptions aren't helping. You aren't helping."

She tried to focus on the documents, to continue her search. Yet her thoughts and emotions tugged her in two directions. The push-pull of wanting to work yet not wanting to work. Wanting Nick. The intimacy, the closeness, the feeling of belonging. Yet not wanting him, not wanting to give up her independence to be with him. Had that been her problem all along?

"Doug brought me to Portland to keep you safe. Not to help build a hotel. Portland has never had a large convention hotel. A little longer won't hurt."

She took a deep breath, deciding how much to tell him so he'd understand. "Norm Talbot, my current boss, wants the financing and land acquisition to go smoothly. And it's not. Something is wrong and it's my job to figure out what. To Talbot this is a very big deal. His father is dangling a VP position in front of him."

"So, what's your role in the process?" He lounged against the end of the couch, looking far too comfortable in her house.

"I have to make sure the legal aspects of the financing are in order. And solve any problems that develop. Which is what I'm trying to do." She gestured toward the page on her screen. "If this project fails, Norm Talbot said he'd fire me." Those last words congealed as a heavy lump in her chest.

"Let me get this straight. You'd jeopardize your life so your boss can get a promotion from his own father and you can keep your job? Who'll do this project if you die?"

A queasy feeling attacked her stomach. "I refuse to think about it. I've worked for the company for over seven years. I can't fail." She put as much determination and fire in those words as she could.

"Okay, then we have to figure out how to keep you safe. Back to the keys." His tone was brusque, business-like.

She heaved a big sigh. "I told the detective I keep my keys in my purse in my locked desk. He was going to check to see if spare keys to the desks are kept secure."

"Doug should know if there's been an answer to that question. Because if he got into your desk, he probably works in the building."

A shudder rippled through her. "Outsiders don't roam in and out of offices."

"Who stops them? The guard at the front door who doesn't check IDs?"

She hesitated. "There's the security cameras."

"Only if they're monitored. Or the videos checked."

"Okay, people do come in from other businesses for meetings and such. I suppose it could be anyone." An admission she was loath to make.

"I'll see if the detective has checked to see if any attempts were made to identify the people seen on the surveillance cameras. He should be able to get the information."

"So what are you trying to do tonight? Besides keep me from working?"

He frowned and shook his head. His sign of exasperation. She hadn't forgotten.

"I need information from you to help us find the guy. What did you tell the detective about the men you've dated lately?"

"I've told him about Andy Pederson so far. He said he'd be questioning me later."

"Okay, that's a starting point. We can speed things up. I want you to make a list of as many men as you can think of that you've had contact with in the past year or so."

"I can't do it. The list would be too long."

"Yes, you can." He handed her a pad and pen. "Start with the guys you've dated, especially the ones you've slept with. List anyone who wanted marriage, like Andy, that you dumped.

Then list anyone who asked you for a date and you refused to go out with them."

She stabbed at the paper with the pen. "You want too much."

"I want as much information as necessary to identify the guy before he grabs you. Help us protect you." He emphasized the last words.

His deep penetrating gaze drew her in. And that queasy feeling returned to her stomach. He was going to strip her bare without touching her. Delve to the core of who she had become. All the intimate details. All her secrets.

CHAPTER 7

*T*ricia wiggled into her corner of the couch, seeking comfort. This was going to be a long evening. She waved the pad at Nick. "Will you question everyone on the list? That could take months."

"We'll narrow our search when we see what we have. The detective will do the questioning. I'll help with computer searches. Doug is coordinating with Chet. Neither the police nor Doug had someone available who could devote twenty-four hours a day to your protection."

She frowned at him, letting all her frustration show. Then she kicked off her shoes and pulled her legs under her. "I don't want around the clock protection. Besides, I didn't think police and private investigators worked together."

"Chet Richardson trusts Doug. They've been friends for years and he respects Doug and values his assistance. And Doug offered to find a bodyguard for you."

"So Doug called you, of all people." Sarcasm crept into her voice.

Nick bristled. "Okay, I realize you don't want me here. You didn't want me around ten years ago, except for the good sex." His expression dared her to deny it.

Her face flushed and the color was surely visible to Nick. She gulped in a breath. "I don't want to discuss the past. What's happening now is what's important."

"Okay. Doug heard I was free, so he called me." A matter-of-fact statement.

She sat up straight, her spine rigid. "Why are you the one free? What does administrative leave mean? Are you under investigation?"

He laughed. "You're questioning me?"

"Why not. You've asked enough questions. My turn."

"Yes, an investigation is standard procedure in an officer involved shooting. They're checking to see if I broke any rules in the drug bust when my partner was killed. I shot two men to save myself and two others."

"Did you break any rules?"

"No. But killing people is taken seriously. And my lieutenant always checks for rule violations."

"I'm sorry about your partner. I shouldn't have pried."

He shrugged. "That's okay. It's information you have a right to, since I'm the one protecting you."

She hesitated, then let her frustration leak into her voice. "Are you sure a list of men I've come into contact with will do you any good?"

"It's a place to start. First, list the men you work with, then the men you've dated. Especially the ones from work you've dated."

"I don't mix business with my private life."

"We don't know how this guy fits into your life. Where he sees you. The one thing we do know for sure, he's a smoker."

"I don't date guys who smoke."

"We can't rule out anyone yet. I've known guys who only smoked on the job, but never at home. Or, the other way around. It's common, with all the restrictions on smoking."

"I still don't think it's anyone I've dated." She set the pad and pen on the couch beside her. "You're expecting me to remember every single man I've come in contact with?"

"As many as you can. This jerk could be someone you see daily and have never paid any attention to. Or someone you've known for a long time."

She winced. "That's an unsettling thought. About three years ago, though, I did go out with an insurance agent who worked in the building and had some dealings with my boss. He came into the office on occasion."

He lifted a brow. "Write down his name."

"I've heard he's married."

"I don't care. Write down his name."

"I just remembered something. Rob Jasper, the insurance guy, had copies of my keys made so he could surprise me with a birthday party at my place. I don't remember him giving those copies to me. He was angry when we broke up and I haven't talked to him since."

"Put him at the top of the list. We'll start with him."

She picked up the pen and the pad and wrote down Rob Jasper, then the first name that came to mind. Then another and another. "This is going to take a long time."

He ran his hand through his hair, mussing it up. Was that a sign of frustration on his part?

"It would help if you also write down how you are acquainted with each guy. Where you met him. Whether you dated. Whether he seemed interested in you. How he looks at you."

She glanced at his disheveled dark hair, that looked like he'd just crawled out of bed. Then brushed that thought away. "A lot of men look at me."

The devilish grin resurfaced. "I like to look at you too."

His words sizzled through her. She gazed at him a moment, at the flash of heat in his eyes. That surprised her.

"While you're working tomorrow, I'll start checking on these guys." His heated gaze slipped away and he pointed to her list. "Give me as much starting info as you can to save me time. I'll make a copy for the detective."

He focused on his laptop, ignoring her. She watched him for a minute then tackled the challenge he'd given her. The damn list.

She quickly dashed off as many names as she could think of, letting her mind conjure up a picture of each of them. She tried to give Nick the kind of details he wanted without revealing too much of herself. The list grew longer while he pounded on his laptop, dealing with email.

She paused the pen on the page. "I don't suppose you want the name of the guy from law school that I dated for a while. He's from the east coast. Long Island."

Nick glanced at her. "Yes, put him on the list. And any last known address."

She added Ben Giordano's name. She'd started dating him because he reminded her of Nick. Italian background. The tall, dark, and handsome cliche. But he'd wanted her to stay in New York and clerk for him at his father's law firm instead of becoming a lawyer herself. She'd dropped him real quick. And refused all dates until she returned to Portland and her new job as a corporate lawyer at Talbot Enterprises.

Finally she flung the pad at him. "I'm finished. If I think of anyone else, I'll add them later." She issued the words as a challenge.

"Thanks." He picked up the pad. "I'll start putting them into a spreadsheet."

The phone rang.

Tricia jumped, then darted from the couch. She stopped before she reached the end table.

"Answer it." Nick stood.

She picked up the phone but didn't hit the talk button.

"Any caller ID?" he asked.

"Wireless caller, no number."

"Hit record on the box the police installed." He pointed to a small black box next to the phone.

She pushed record, then the talk button on the phone. "Hello." She said it quietly, then held her breath.

"Get that man out of your house. You're mine." She gripped the phone tighter. His tone was low, growling, menacing. The shaking began in her hands and raced up her arms and into her chest. She couldn't breathe. She couldn't think.

He hung up.

"He's outside." She whispered the words. Then pushed the off button on the phone and set the receiver down, like it was contaminated. She stared at the wall and willed herself to get control. But control was so far gone.

Nick pulled her into his arms and cradled her to his chest. She burrowed closer, needing his warmth and support. "He knows you're here." Her voice came out as a small squeak. "He was watching when we came in."

She squirmed in his grasp and shook her head. "I didn't want to believe it."

"You get it now, don't you?"

An icy chill sped down her spine. "Yes. I get it. I need to

cooperate with you and Doug and the police. Whether it's convenient or not, I'm in danger."

~

Tricia's familiar scent teased Nick, kindling memories. When she tried to wiggle out of his arms, he tightened his grip on her. His body remembered how it felt to hold her. For a moment he let the sensations cascade through him, igniting flames deep within.

The rapid beat of her heart against his chest brought him out of his sensual haze. She'd had a scare. He tried for a gentle tone, to soothe her. "Stay here. I want to hear what he said."

He reached over and pushed the button to turn on the recording. Anger flared in his gut. The man's voice was pure menace. "This jerk is not going to get his hands on you."

Her pale face and wary eyes wrenched his heart. He'd give anything to get rid of this guy and give her back a normal life. He hurt, seeing her like this. "I should have made sure there were two phones in the room."

"He could have been outside the whole time." Her voice was shaky.

"I didn't see anyone hanging around when we came inside. And we don't know what he'll do next, since I'm not leaving."

She shoved him away, like she was startled to find herself in his arms. "So what does a frustrated stalker do when he can't get to his victim?"

"The key word is frustrated—how frustrated he gets. For now you're safe." He retreated a few feet, far enough to dull the effects of her intoxicating scent. "The guy doesn't know who I am or why I'm here with you. He won't break in. His goal is to get you alone."

"He may have seen us coming out of the Talbot building or the restaurant." Her voice was stronger, more confident. "If he's following me. Depends on how smart he is."

"Oh, he's smart."

She sank onto the couch. "He may be a smoker, but he didn't stay in here long enough to smoke. The odor probably came off his clothes." Her expression brightened. "Maybe he smoked while he was outside. And left some butts behind."

"Whoa." He picked up the phone and dialed Chet's number. "You're thinking better than I am."

She got up from the couch. "I'm going to make a pot of coffee. This is going to be a long evening. You want some?" She headed for the kitchen.

He called after her. "Yeah, coffee sounds good." She seemed to have recovered from the trauma of the call. Thinking of the cigarette butts helped.

Chet answered immediately. "Nick Castellani here. Our suspect was outside watching the house. He called and Tricia picked up the phone and heard his voice. He knows I'm with her and doesn't like it. Someone should check the perimeter for fresh cigarette butts."

Nick ended the call, then joined Tricia in the kitchen. "Chet's coming himself to check for fresh butts outside. I had another thought. What if he works during the day and only stalks you at night? Could be he doesn't know why I'm here and he's worried. But that wouldn't explain how he got your keys."

He leaned against the counter as Tricia poured water into the machine and measured coffee into the basket.

"Did Doug tell you he has someone in the office who's a skilled tech they use for online searches? Erik could help with those names."

"I'll see Doug tomorrow morning. I'll ask about the tech." He sat on the stool at the bar separating the kitchen from the dining room. Its granite top matched the countertops in the kitchen and blended with the flooring.

"Was the kitchen already remodeled when you bought this house?"

"Yes. I think I fell in love with the house because of the kitchen. And the big bathtub upstairs in my bathroom."

"I can see why. The house suits you." A stylish house to go with a stylish woman. Another phone rested on a charger on a cabinet. "How many phones do you have on the line?"

"Four. We can take this one into the living room. I'll get the spare from my office later." She picked up the phone from the charger.

When the coffee was ready, they carried their cups to the living room and settled on the couch. Tricia picked up the list and added four more names. Then tossed it to him.

Nick clicked on his browser and checked two databases he had access to through his police work. No one showed up with an arrest record, either state or federal. Damn. This guy wasn't going to make it easy for them.

His cell phone rang. Tricia jumped, then fell back against the couch with a startled expression.

He picked up the phone. "It's Doug."

She visibly calmed.

He answered.

"Nick. I'm checking in to see what's happening. Is everything okay tonight?"

Nick hesitated a moment. "No. The guy called here a little while ago. He saw us together and doesn't like it. He wants me out of here."

"No clues, I assume."

"There could be, outside. Chet is checking for discarded cigarette butts."

"Good thinking. That could be our break."

"Tricia thought of it. I don't like what he's saying. I don't like that he's outside her house, even when I'm inside with her."

"So what are you going to do?" Doug's tone was demanding.

"I've asked Tricia for a list of names of guys she comes in contact with. I'd like to use your computer tech to help research them. I wish there was an easy way to find out who smokes and who doesn't. Someone will have to question these guys."

"Erik can do online searches for you. Chet will do the questioning, so any information you can give him will help. Come to the office after you take her to work in the morning. Then you can catch me up on what you have."

"Okay. See you tomorrow." He hung up.

Tricia hadn't said anything, simply sipped her coffee while he talked to Doug.

He set down his phone. "Let's quit for tonight. Too much has happened."

She frowned at him and reached for her laptop. "I brought home work I have to do. These interruptions haven't helped. You play detective while I concentrate on what I need to get done before tomorrow." She opened a file on the screen, shutting him out.

She focused on the document in front of her. He admired her tenacity. She'd get through this. Hell, she'd graduated from law school and had a high powered job as a corporate lawyer.

His job here in Portland was to keep her alive and safe. When the guy was caught, he'd return to his job in L.A. And leave a piece of his heart behind.

CHAPTER 8

*A*fter an hour the figures on the spreadsheet appeared as a scrambled mess. Tricia couldn't figure out what was the bigger cause. The knot of fear that squeezed her heart and kept her breathing shallow. Or Nick on the other end of the couch.

The fear had been with her for two whole days, since her home had been invaded. It gnawed at her insides and chilled her until she thought she'd never warm up. She shuddered, then glanced at Nick.

Since he'd showed up yesterday evening, he'd muddled her concentration and stirred up thoughts she shouldn't be having.

She'd actually considered abandoning her own dreams to go with him to L.A. Until she came to her senses, the night of the big argument. The big argument that reinforced her view that men couldn't be trusted.

She focused on the spreadsheet, shutting out everything else, until her lower back screamed in protest. She straightened and stretched. Sitting on the couch, bending over the coffee table, was not the most comfortable position for working.

"Need a back rub?" He said the words innocently enough. She'd been the recipient of many back rubs from Nick that had escalated into something far more satisfying.

"No." She kept her focus on the spreadsheet, and tried to ignore Nick.

"Something wrong?"

"Yes. These figures don't balance." She pointed at the offending spreadsheet. "I found an early copy of the file that shows the place where the missing bid should be. Whoever took the figures out of the file erased their trail. It's as if the bid had never been entered."

"You can't find the problem?" He gazed intently at her, empathy in those dark eyes.

He did care. He was trying to help. "Someone doesn't want me to find it. Paperwork from the file on the server is missing. And I haven't found any traces yet in the stack of papers I scanned before I left the office."

"Anything else you can do tonight?" That same intense gaze.

"Not much. When I get to the office tomorrow, I'll make some calls, to see if I can find someone who'll tell me what's going on."

"Do you think the problems are deliberate?"

She leaned back against the couch and stretched again. "Yes. My instincts tell me someone has used devious means to cover up whatever was done. Possibly so I'm the one who gets the blame when the project fails."

"Protecting their own jobs."

"Could be. The financing was in place, they said over and over. Yet one investor pulled his financing, and all traces of the missing bid have been wiped out. Deliberately."

"Good luck." He said it with compassion. Compassion echoed in his expression. Then he focused on his computer.

She stared at the spreadsheet on her own computer. Corporate law had dull moments, but overall she enjoyed the work and was good at it. Usually facts and figures didn't lie. Didn't cheat. Didn't go away and leave you. Her mother never learned that lesson. Tricia never forgot it.

And now something was wrong with the figures. They were lying too. Work imitating life. Complications piled one on top of another.

Her focus drifted, but she doggedly resisted gazing at Nick. He was pounding on his laptop keyboard. Doug wouldn't have brought him up here if he hadn't thought Nick could help. And if she examined her true feelings, she was glad for his protection.

But he dominated any room he was in. Never mind she'd been inches from falling in love with him when she'd moved clear across the country to go to law school. Ten years and he still turned her on with a glance or a touch. But above all else, she enjoyed the warm, fuzzy feeling of contentment being with him gave her.

When she did look up, Nick was staring at her.

"Doug said your mother died, that you're all alone. No family here except for Doug and his mother." He said the words quietly, like he didn't want to upset her.

"My mother died five years ago. Cancer. I miss her." She felt the words deep down inside, a sharp stab of pain. Even though she and her mother were never close, the void was there.

"But your father is alive."

"He was never much of a father. I haven't seen him since I was ten. He never comes here. Never sends a birthday card or a Christmas card. I don't even have his latest address."

"That must hurt."

She did hurt. Her father never loved her, never showed her any affection. But she wouldn't admit that to Nick. "My father was horrible to my mother. She loved him and he betrayed her. She never trusted another man after he left."

"Is that why you haven't married? You're afraid a man won't stay around?"

"No. I want to be independent, and do what I want to do without having to consider the needs of another person." She shrugged. "It's that simple."

"I don't buy it. You're afraid and you won't admit it. You rejected what we could have had, because you thought I'd do the same to you. You got scared when I asked you to go to Los Angeles with me."

"No. No. That's not it. I had a scholarship to law school in New York. I was thinking about myself and my own career."

"There was more to it." Nick was standing in front of her, his expression guarded.

She hugged her body as she let the memories of her childhood filter through her consciousness. Maybe she was a bit defensive because of her father. But she wasn't going to admit it to Nick. She'd made up her mind a long time ago she'd never need a man like her mother had needed her father. He'd let her down. No man would do that to her. She was too afraid of losing herself.

She pushed thoughts of her father aside, the way she'd trained herself to do. The hurt ran too deep.

Yet she wanted Nick. They'd had good sex. She wanted more. But she had enough problems without adding sex with Nick to the mix. She would enjoy his company while he was here to protect her. Then she'd let him go. For a second time.

"I'll get us more coffee." He picked up their cups.

But coffee wasn't what she wanted. She wanted the comfort of being in his arms. When he sat down beside her and handed her the refilled cup, his fingers brushed hers. She gripped the cup tightly to keep from dropping it, and gazed into the dark depths of his eyes. He took a drink, then set his cup down and reached for hers, setting it on the coffee table beside his.

Then he leaned toward her. She read the intent on his face. A kiss would be disastrous, utterly change their situation. Yet her body desperately wanted the kiss he promised. Her mind was equally desperate. And afraid. And told her no.

Her mind won.

She scooted over on the couch and shut off her computer, then stood. "No. I'm going to bed. Alone." She fled up the stairs.

TRICIA ROUNDED the corner into the kitchen and grasped the door jamb to stop herself. Nick sat at the table, eating a bowl of cereal. Nervous flutters invaded her stomach. She'd never before let a man spend an entire night at her house.

Her dreams had been about Nick, about wanting to make love to him. She woke up before she found out if they did end up in bed together. She wanted the kiss she'd turned down.

"Don't run off." He raised his head and his eyes radiated compassion. "Better eat something." His words were quiet. "I'm sorry. I was out of line last night."

A slight scowl etched his face and his eyes had a wariness she hadn't seen before.

"I came here to protect you, not seduce you."

"Uh, thanks." She wasn't sure if she felt relief, or regret.

What did she truly want? Her precious independence. Which meant never having Nick.

She breathed in the aroma of fresh coffee. Then grabbed a cereal bowl from the cupboard, along with a cup. The jolt of caffeine helped and she ate her breakfast, trying not to think about Nick sitting in the chair directly across the table from her. Close, yet a wall of sorts between them.

After a quick cleanup of the kitchen, they gathered their things and met at the front door.

"Let's go." She tried for a brusque tone. His devilish smile implied he could tell what she was thinking.

She opened the front door and let out a shriek. Her hand brushed something crimson and wet. Nick gripped her arm and pulled her inside, tucking her behind him. He drew his gun from under his jacket, opened the door a crack, and peered outside. Then stepped out the door.

Her pulse pounded. Nick was a cop. She was seeing a side of him she'd never glimpsed before.

Full bodyguard mode.

He came back inside. "Red paint. Still wet. He was here a short time ago."

She looked closely at her hand, at the red streak where she'd touched the side of the door. Paint. Not blood. "I'll go wash this off."

She scrubbed the red from her hand at the kitchen sink. Back at the front door, it was obvious the stripe was red paint. A bright red slash across the middle of the door.

Her stomach clenched and rage soared through her. Her stalker had been on the front porch this morning. Earlier in the week he'd been bold enough to get inside and leave the awful message. This time he'd damaged the outside of the solid oak front door.

"He's letting you know he can get close even when I'm here. I hope he assumes I'm a boyfriend."

A lump settled in her throat. This couldn't be happening. He'd been outside when they were sleeping. Thank goodness Nick was in the house with her, though in a different room and a different bed. At least Nick could have protected her if the guy had wanted to do more than send a message. Her safe little world had disappeared.

"I need to call someone to get this door refinished." Her voice was tentative. Not her usual take charge manner.

"Make the call from the office. I'll call Chet and tell him what happened. Let's get you to work."

Nick locked the dead bolt from the outside, then grasped her arm and steered her down the steps. "Yes, it's serious. Yes, you're in danger."

THE ELEVATOR DOOR CLOSED, blocking Tricia's view of Nick. She turned and her spirits plummeted. Andy Pederson stood in the foyer between her and the office corridor. Another complication to add to another already complicated day.

His insincere smile and raised chin told her everything there was to know about the man. His ego was in charge. She stiffened her spine. His blond heart-throb looks would not get him what he wanted today.

He hadn't taken their breakup well, but her usual guilty conscience was buried deep where Andy was concerned. That made getting rid of him easier. He'd left several messages for her on her phone, after she'd told him to stop.

Rather than barge by him to get to her office, she'd put an end to her dealings with him today and cross one more item off her to-do list. She stopped in front of him, keeping her briefcase between them as a barrier.

"Hi, Tricia. I'm taking you to lunch today. I have something to discuss with you."

"No, Andy. No lunch. No discussion. We said what we needed to say last month."

"Maybe you said what you wanted to. This time you're going to listen to me."

"There's absolutely nothing you could say that will change my mind."

"We'll talk about it over lunch."

"No we won't. I have too much work to do. No time for lunch out." *And I'm not trusting anyone right now.* Of course she wouldn't tell him that. He wasn't her stalker. He didn't have access to her office. He worked in another building down the block.

Yet he was on the eighth floor, standing outside the Talbot offices, in the Talbot building.

She remembered something the detective had said. *Nothing is impossible if a criminal is determined.*

"Make time. I have something to say to you." He used the same commanding tone she'd come to associate with him when they'd dated. The tone that had grated on her then, sounded menacing today.

"No. I meant what I said. I won't go out with you again. We are finished." She sidestepped around him. "I'm late. I have to get to my office." She escaped into the hallway.

She viewed every man with suspicion. Especially ones she'd dumped. Except Nick. He was one of the good guys, yet he had the potential to hurt her the most.

CHAPTER 9

*D*oug was on the phone when Nick arrived at his office. That gave him a chance to think about the unsettling news he'd heard from Eddie Velasquez.

Doug waved him to a chair and continued his conversation. When he ended the call, he swiveled to face Nick.

"Something happened." Doug's tone was accusatory, with a tinge of hostility thrown in.

"Are you asking me if something happened?"

"You're worried. I can tell by your expression. Is it Tricia?" His gaze bore into Nick.

"No, not Tricia. She's safely at work. Did your investigator, Alison, make it back to Portland?" In the past he would have countered with an accusation or sarcasm. Their conversations weren't always cordial.

"She's driving so it will take her a couple of days."

"When did she leave L.A.?"

"Yesterday. Soon after I called her. Why?"

"I got a message from Velasquez about thirty minutes ago.

She must have gone where she shouldn't. Moreno was told she was there and somehow he knew she's connected to you. He's added her to his hit list."

"Oh, shit. She was in her old neighborhood when I called her."

"And you're sure she left town?"

"She was in her car at a hamburger place and said she would leave immediately. She'd wanted to see old acquaintances. I should have reminded her before she left here of the dangers of going into Moreno's territory. Times have changed." He picked up his cell phone and sent a text message. "If she's on the road, she'll answer when she can." He set the cell phone on his desk where he could see if a response came through.

Doug's concerned expression and the tightness in his voice told Nick that Alison might be more than an employee. Maybe Doug had moved beyond the loss of his wife. Or maybe Nick wanted to make more out of this than warranted. Probably the last option.

"What else did Velasquez say?"

"You're at the top of his hit list. He's coming after you himself."

"You told me that. But not when." A demanding tone.

Nick snickered, though not in amusement. "You don't think he'll give you a date, do you?"

Doug glanced at the window behind him.

"Yeah, maybe you shouldn't sit in front of a window. Perfect target."

Doug scowled, his dark eyebrows almost coming together. "I'll make some changes before he gets here." He hesitated. "Why is Moreno still in L.A., if he wants to expand his business into the northwest?"

"His organization isn't big enough to satisfy him yet. Word is he's further cementing his ties to the narcos in Mexico. He'll need a larger, steadier supply of cocaine, heroin, and meth from the cartels for his expansion plans."

"What area is he targeting in L.A.?"

"He's after Lopez and his territory in south central. Moreno lost the four years he spent in Mexico after you busted up his gang and seized that heroin shipment and that five million dollars in cash. Of course he blames you for that, as well as the death of his sons. Once he rebuilds his turf, getting rid of you becomes his next priority." Nick kept his tone as objective as he could while he seethed inside.

"Let me know as soon as you hear anything from Velasquez." Doug's voice held a hint of worry.

"Of course."

Doug's expression changed to puzzled. "What about the situation with Tricia?"

"More trouble. The guy put a stripe of red paint on Tricia's front door in the early hours this morning."

Doug shook his head and scrunched his eyes. An expression Nick recognized as Doug's signature frustration mode. "Did you call Chet?"

"Yes."

"That was him on the phone. He's picking up the report on Tricia's locks before coming here."

"At least we'll have the information this morning."

"There's more, but I'll get to it in a minute. What's going on with Tricia? Is she ready to accept your help?"

Nick hesitated. Something else in Doug's expression, his rigid features, his taut mouth, had Nick concerned. "I think she will. She wants to believe she can take care of herself. But the guy has her scared. He got inside her house. He called last night. He put the paint on the door this morning. She finally believes that he plans to kill her." He punctuated his words with a shake of his head.

"That's always been his plan." Doug's retort was swift.

"Yeah, and the SOB wants us to know he's around. Yet his actions don't make sense. He has to realize she won't be left alone. He knew I was in the house when he called. He told her to get rid of me. 'You're mine,' he said."

"His behavior is irrational. He could snap."

"At any time." Nick rubbed his chin. "Last night, after the guy called, I mentioned her mother and her father. She said she hadn't seen her father since she was ten."

Doug winced. "I haven't seen my daughters since they were younger than that."

"Different situation. Their lives could have been in danger. Adam is avoiding Tricia, when he could be a part of her life. How can two brothers be so unlike?"

"We had different mothers, didn't grow up together, and he's ten years older."

"How's your mother doing?"

"She still lives in the house where I grew up. She's content with her life." Doug's smile underlined his deep affection for his mother. Then his expression darkened. "Tricia should take a vacation. Leave town."

"She won't do it. The project she's working on has problems. A big convention hotel for Portland with complicated financial negotiations. And a missing bid. It's her boss's pet project. Her job's on the line."

"Her life is more important." Doug's tone was emphatic. "Starting today, she's not going to that office building without you there too. I'm calling her boss. Stick with her."

"She'll object."

"Let her object. I'll also request a security tour for you, since

Chet hasn't had the time to go there. You can assess the situation before you show up at her office."

Doug stared at his mute phone, then stood and limped around to the front of the desk. He leaned against the desk. "Before I make the call to her boss, what exactly about security do you want to see for yourself?"

Nick stood too. "Where the surveillance cameras are located in the areas where she'll be and where the monitors are, and if they are watched or how the recordings are reviewed."

"What have you seen so far?"

"The guy at the front door. Two cameras in the lobby. Another camera in the hallway outside Tricia's office."

"Okay, I'll make the arrangements. If her boss wants her to keep working, he'll have to agree. I'll check with building management about the security tour."

"This is going to be an interesting day." Sarcasm rode the edge of Nick's words.

"We'll do what we have to do to keep her safe." Doug's expression lightened. "Now the good news. Chet found three fresh cigarette butts on the sidewalk near her house. He's requested expedited DNA testing as an emergency. He's also questioning neighbors to see if anyone saw the guy outside her house."

"How long does expedited mean around here?"

"It could be two or three days, if we're lucky. He's getting the FBI involved as much as possible, since the guy could have killed in other places. In the meantime, we can beef up her security." Doug's pointed stare was etched with a challenge. "You're her personal bodyguard around the clock."

"She'll resent it. But she can continue to work. Her choice."

"Okay, let's try it. Take your laptop to the office with you and work on what you can."

A quick knock, then the door opened.

"Come on in, Chet." Doug motioned to the older man at the door. "This is Nick Castellani, who's guarding Tricia." Doug limped to his chair behind the desk.

Nick greeted Chet.

"Hi, Nick." Chet extended his hand and Nick took it. "I wanted to meet you in person, so I don't shoot the wrong guy, if there's a shoot-out."

"Hey, good thinking. Neither of us wear uniforms. Glad to meet you too."

"A perk of being a detective." Chet glanced down at his slacks and sport coat. "We get to look like civilians." He stepped back and assessed Nick. "I would have recognized you anyway. You're definitely your father's son. How old were you when he got hit?"

"Sixteen."

"The kid on meth who shot him couldn't have been much older than you were. I was sorry to lose your dad, as a fellow officer and a friend."

A stab of grief hit Nick. "Thanks. I wish I could have had more time with him as I was growing up. Mom never got over his death."

"So, how did she accept you becoming a cop too?"

Nick grimaced. "She tried her best to talk me out of it. So I took a job in L.A where Doug was then. She decided to move to Virginia, to be close to my sister."

"Do you ever think about returning to Portland?"

"Yes. I miss it. I didn't realize how much until after I got here." He laughed. "I even like the rain."

"Well, let's get down to business." Chet sat in one chair in front of the desk and Nick sat in the other. "I'm on my way to an appointment with the FBI special agent who's been assigned to this case. We're searching for a tie in with other murders in other states. He's the one who's helping get the DNA on the cigarette butts processed quickly. By the way, the locks were not picked, unless the guy's a total expert. No scratches beyond regular wear."

"What we expected." Nick nodded. "The door was locked when Tricia got home."

"What about the keys to the desks in the Talbot Building?" Doug asked.

"Each company keeps its own keys," Chet said. "In her office area the keys are in a cabinet that is normally locked, but lots of people have access."

"So anyone could have gotten the key to her desk." Nick frowned. "That in itself says something about the security in that building.

"The DNA from the cigarette butts may give us something to go on."

"We need a name." Nick's words were emphatic.

"We can't count on finding one," Doug said. "Do you have copies of Tricia's list?"

"No, but I have my flash drive with me."

"Let me make copies."

Nick took the flash drive out of his briefcase and handed it to Doug. Doug accessed his computer and quickly made four copies. He handed one to Chet. "I'll keep copies for myself and Erik."

He handed the other one to Nick, along with the flash drive. "Erik is a whiz. He'll find what you only dreamed of finding."

"I certainly hope so. And the police should have even more resources."

"We do." Chet put his copy in the folder he carried. "I'm

picking up a roster of employees of businesses in the Talbot Building, including support staff. We'll run the names."

"Maybe we'll get a break."

Chet checked his watch. "I'll be late for my appointment if I don't leave. Keep me informed of anything you find. I'll do the same. With everyone working on it, we ought to narrow the list quickly."

When the door closed behind Chet, Doug glanced first at the phone on his desk. Then at Nick.

"What?"

"Yeah. One more question. You and Tricia were in a relationship for a couple of years. Will that create a problem?"

Nick hesitated, feeling guilty over the kiss he wanted last night but didn't get. His momentary lapse. "I honestly can't say. She's uncomfortable with me there. She dumped me to go off to law school. I was hurt. I'm over it."

"Was your relationship serious?"

"On my part. Evidently not hers."

"Adam's fault, for the rotten way he treated her mother. She protects herself by hurting first. I've seen that happen a few times."

Nick thought of their discussion the night before and her denial. "So Andy's the latest and I was one of the early ones."

"Her pool of rejected lovers is a good place to start looking for your suspect."

"Check your list. Did she leave anyone off who should be there?"

Doug scanned the page on the desk in front of him. "Rob Jasper has a set of her keys? She broke up with him more than three years ago. There was something about him I didn't like."

"Can you give me anything on any of the other guys on her list?"

Doug studied the page. "I'll jot notes when I think of something."

Nick put his copy in his briefcase.

"Go introduce yourself to Erik, middle door on the right, then go to Tricia's office and by then I'll have contacted her boss, Norm Talbot. His dad, Jerome Talbot, is an okay guy, but this son is ambitious and could cause us trouble."

"The choice is his, if he wants her to keep working."

Nick headed for the door. "Tricia is not going to like having me in her office with her."

"You'll get the brunt of her anger." For the first time today Doug's features softened and hinted of a sincere smile. "She's one determined woman when she has her mind made up." Pride shown through in the tone of his voice.

"So I've discovered." Nick struggled to stay objective. His own feelings about Tricia were getting more complicated by the day. And night.

CHAPTER 10

*N*ick located the security office in the Talbot
Building tucked in behind the lobby on the first
floor. Dan Hix, head of security, took him to the surveillance
room on the second floor. Monitors, projecting various images,
covered two walls and extended to a third. Maybe the situation
wasn't as bad as he had feared.

"That's Roger Mobley watching the monitors." Hix gestured
toward the monitors, which showed many angles of the
building and the hallways, including the two views of the lobby.
"He's on duty during the day while the building is occupied.
Louie Mendez takes over for the evening, and stays until
midnight. The feeds are recorded."

Mobley glanced at Nick, then at the monitors without
acknowledging him.

Nick pointed at the monitors. "Which is the view of the
eighth floor hallway?"

Mobley pointed to a monitor on the side wall, about in the
middle. "There's two. The one on the right is from the camera

by the conference room and the other is near the reception desk."

Nick found the feeds Mobley indicated, though he couldn't see the door to Tricia's office. "It looks like everything is covered." He said the words to Hix. Though he didn't mean it. Too many holes in their security.

"Like I told you. We have a good system. Roger there will let us know if anything is wrong. Then the police are called immediately."

"Good enough." Nick followed the older man out of the room.

"We'll take a shortcut to the eighth floor." Hix unlocked an unmarked door. "This is the service corridor."

Once inside, they walked down a concrete hallway with numerous doors. Their footsteps echoed throughout the corridor. Uneasiness stirred in Nick's gut.

Hix used a key to open an elevator that took them to the eighth floor, into another service corridor. From the doorway across from the elevator, they emerged into the hallway a short distance from Tricia's office.

The uneasiness in his gut intensified. On the other side of that door they'd come through was a warren of corridors, hidden from the cameras. And a private service elevator. He'd mention the hidden corridors to Doug and Chet later.

Hix then escorted him on a tour of the area where Tricia worked, Talbot Enterprises. He pointed out the location of the cameras in the hallway near Tricia's office.

Nick located the camera near Tricia's office door. It was aimed down the hall. "Could that camera be shifted so it records not only who's in the hallway but also who goes in and out of Tricia's office?"

"Sure. I'll see to it today. Anything else?"

"Not now. Thanks for the tour."

"If you need anything else, call me," Hix said.

Nick said goodbye to Hix and headed for the open door of Tricia's office. Steeling himself for an angry reception.

TRICIA TENSED. Someone had entered her office behind her. She swiveled in her chair. Nick stood just inside the door, briefcase in hand.

First surprise, then anger spiked through her. What was he doing here? This was not where he belonged. Not in her office.

He wore a wary expression.

"Is something wrong?"

"Doug ordered twenty-four hour protection for you. Talbot said okay, though grudgingly. You're not to be left alone until this guy is caught." His words were delivered in a flat tone, no inflection, without emotion.

Her anger ignited into a firestorm inside her body. "Don't I have anything to say about it?"

"No. I'm your bodyguard. I'm here for your safety."

How could she concentrate with him in the room? She had enough trouble last night. "You can't stay here while I'm working." She tried to keep the panic out of her voice.

"I certainly can, and I will."

"The stalker isn't coming after me here. He's not going to do something to bring attention to himself."

Nick walked closer. "Until he's ready to grab you." He kept his words quiet, but forceful. "We have no idea who he is or where he is during the day, which means anyone who's around you could be a suspect. So I stay close."

His scowl dared her to argue further. He sat on the chair

87

next to a small table and took his laptop out of his briefcase, along with several file folders and a pen. "Where's a plug for my A/C adapter?"

With an angry glance, she pointed to a wall outlet three feet behind him. He plugged in and returned to his seat, ignoring her.

Then he inserted a USB modem into his computer and logged onto the internet. And accessed email. Then he stopped and looked up. "I thought you had work to do."

"I do. I'm searching for a way to save the project, if it's possible." She swiveled around to her desk, and clicked into the file. "If I can't figure this out, I'm going to lose my job." The threat was as real as her stalker.

TRICIA LEANED against the passenger seat of the SUV. A dull ache pulsed in her forehead. They'd stopped for dinner on the way home. This evening she wanted to relax, far from Nick. The taut nerves in her entire body screamed for release. As soon as she was inside, she'd escape to her room.

They rounded the corner onto her street and she gasped. The throbbing in her forehead intensified. Three police cars with lights flashing sat in the street in front of her house.

The front gate and the front door stood wide open. Chet Richardson, the detective she'd talked to the first night, was on the porch, gesturing to an officer in uniform.

"What's going on?" Resignation permeated her words.

"We'll find out soon." Nick parked in the driveway, behind her car. They got out of the SUV.

Tricia glanced at the neighbors who'd spilled out of the

apartment building across the street, attracted by the drama unfolding. She hurried up the steps.

"Was it our guy? How did he get in?" Nick had switched to an all-business tone. Forceful, authoritative.

"He cut through the screen and the window glass in the laundry room," Chet said. "The cop on patrol spotted the break-in, but the guy was gone."

"Another message?"

"A huge one."

Nick scowled. "I don't like the sound of that."

Tricia's chest tightened and her breath caught. Must be something worse than the original message.

Chet led the way inside. Tricia detected a faint odor of cigarette smoke. Anger coiled in her midsection. Along with frustration.

The ache in her head pounded harder. The pillows on the couch had been slashed open, their stuffing littering the floor. A trail of red paint on the carpet led up the stairway. She slumped against the wall in the foyer, too paralyzed to move.

"What else has he done?" She forced out the words.

"Plenty." The grim look on Chet's face scared her.

"I'm going to need an alarm system that alerts the police."

"We'll get one installed, before you spend another night in this house." Doug's voice came from behind her. She hadn't heard him arrive.

"You won't be able to stay here tonight," Chet said.

"I want to see what else he did." She clipped the words, trying to keep her voice strong even as her backbone threatened to crumble.

"Maybe you shouldn't." Chet's words held compassion. "It's going to take a professional team to do the cleanup. Your bedroom is literally destroyed."

Her chest constricted and the pain spread throughout her body. "I have to see it. No matter how bad. I can't leave without knowing what he's done. Otherwise my imagination will keep me awake tonight." Though nightmares might also ruin her sleep.

"All right. Take her upstairs, Nick. Don't touch anything," Chet said. "The house will be dusted for fingerprints."

She plodded up the stairs, avoiding the stripe of paint on the carpet. Nick stayed right behind her.

At the doorway to her bedroom, she stopped. She shuddered and tremors cascaded through her body. Her clothes were piled in the middle of the floor, sliced to ribbons. What was left of her favorite camel-colored cashmere sweater sat on top with holes cut out where her breasts would have been.

Nick pulled her into his arms. "Don't look anymore. I don't like the message sent by the mutilated sweater. This guy is dangerous." His mouth was set in a grim line.

She closed her eyes and took solace in the warmth of his embrace. For only a moment. Then she opened her eyes and surveyed the damage. Her bed had been slashed open, through the mattress and into the box springs. The mirror over her dresser had a lipstick message, the same one as in the bathroom the last time. "Then you die," was in larger letters than "You're mine."

Her knees buckled and Nick tightened his grasp and kept her from falling. "You're not going to faint, are you?"

"I had a headache when we got here. My head feels like it's being squeezed in a vise. I'm weak."

"Sit on the edge of the bed."

"No. I've got to get out of here."

Downstairs in the living room, she sank onto a chair not

littered with the stuffing from the pillows. Doug and Chet and one officer were talking in the foyer.

Chet saw her and walked over. "Before you leave, I want you to go back upstairs and check your jewelry boxes, to see if anything is missing."

"Okay. Any particular reason?"

"The FBI profiler requested the information. I'll ask why when I talk to him." He ambled back to where Doug and the officer waited.

She stood. "Before I go upstairs, I need a drink of water and something for this pain."

"I'll get the water for you," Nick said.

"No. I can do that much for myself." She scowled at him and headed for the kitchen. He followed and waited until she'd swallowed the aspirin she'd taken from a cupboard. Then he opened his arms wide. She walked into his arms and melted into the comfort.

"I'm so sorry." He cradled her gently.

When she gazed up at him, she saw the concern in his dark eyes, and the worry lines on his forehead. Did he really care? The man she had wounded so badly when they were younger? His actions so far seemed to indicate he did care.

THE DOOR of the hotel suite clicked shut behind them. Tricia exhaled and her shoulders sagged. "How safe are we here? Could he have followed us?"

"It's possible. Though we did have a police escort while we shopped for the things you needed for the night." Nick set down his suitcase and two shopping bags in the middle of the room.

"I didn't see anyone." She set down the two shopping bags she held.

"Good. That means she was doing her job right. She was watching for anyone watching us."

"So, if we weren't followed, I'm safe for one more night." Even she could hear the lack of conviction in her tone. She swiveled around and checked out the suite. They were in the sitting room. Two bedroom doors stood open. The drapes were drawn at the windows. A very typical hotel. Nondescript. Functional.

"Yes, we're safe. Doug arranged for this suite so our names aren't on record at the front desk. The guy will have to find us another way."

"Or wait until tomorrow, when I'm at the office."

"And I'll be with you wherever you are."

"I'm in total shock. He destroyed everything in my bedroom, except my jewelry. Then stole my two favorite pieces, ones with sentimental value."

"Have you told anyone you dated what the pearls and bracelet meant to you?"

"I don't remember telling anyone. I didn't wear the pearls much. They were old-fashioned, but my mother gave them to me when I graduated from high school. I bought the diamond bracelet after I passed the bar exams." Her heart constricted at the thought that an unknown man had her treasures.

Surely he wasn't aware of their significance. Unless he was someone who knew her well. That thought was even more unnerving.

She stood in the middle of the room, clutching her briefcase and her purse. Her body and mind numb. "It's getting worse."

"He's frustrated. He may make a mistake. Then we nab him."

"If he doesn't get to me first." She dropped her purse, brief-case, and coat on a sofa.

Nick crossed the room and gathered her into his arms, holding her tightly. She squirmed, then stopped. The warmth and caring in his grasp held her in place. Gave her a moment's respite from the fear.

"He's not going to get to you. I promise." His breath was warm on her neck.

"How can you promise? You don't have any more idea who he is than I do." She mumbled the words into his shirt.

"We're doing what we can to find him and keep you safe. I'm not leaving your side."

That warmth of his body next to hers was too familiar. Felt too good. Panic built inside her. She shoved him, a little too hard. He stumbled.

"I'm going to put away my things." She picked up her bags, and ran for the nearest bedroom.

CHAPTER 11

Tricia dropped her purse and briefcase on her office desk, then snatched them up. A shudder rushed through her and her arms and shoulders started shaking. "Nick!" A deep gash snaked down the middle of the oak surface of the desk. Red paint oozed from the slash.

Nick grasped her arms from behind and steered her away from the desk. She set her purse and briefcase on the chair by the wall. Nick turned her around and held her to his chest. She burrowed closer, still shaking.

Self-preservation kicked in and she squirmed out of the warmth, the strength, of his grasp. "I'm okay. The shock. Seeing that..."

"So much for the security in this building." Nick let her go, but his harsh demeanor told her he was angry and barely holding it in. He picked up the phone on her desk. "I'm calling the police. I'm not going through building security. I don't trust them."

Tricia sank into another chair across from her desk and

listened to his side of the conversation. The guy wasn't letting up.

Nick finished his call. "He's trying to spook you."

"He's succeeded." She took a deep breath, to steady herself. "I'm not safe in my house or my office. Is that the message he's sending me?"

"I'd say it's the message he's sending everyone." Nick punched in another number on his phone. "I'm calling Doug while we wait for the police. Have the receptionist summon Talbot."

Norm Talbot stormed into the room ten minutes later, his usual grim expression firmly in place. Two police officers followed him in. Tricia stood to face Talbot.

"Ms. Landreth, take your files and work at home today while this desk is repaired. Use email and phone to stay in touch. No more interruptions. You will be here Monday morning, ready to work."

Nick confronted Talbot. "Something is wrong with the security in this building."

"She's the cause of the disruption, not security." He frowned at Tricia. "Do the job you were assigned, or you'll be replaced." He left the office.

Tricia retreated to the chair by the wall. The officers checked out the desk and asked Nick questions. She had intended to go see several people today and get answers to her questions. People with knowledge of what was going on in the finance department. When she was not in the office, she'd have to use the phone or email and couldn't see their reactions, couldn't gauge whether or not they were telling the truth or lying.

And she couldn't shake the feeling that Talbot wanted her out of the office, far from anyone with answers.

"Nick, before we leave here, go with me to the finance department. To see if someone will talk to me."

"No. Let's get you out of here." His tone was emphatic.

"Okay." Again, her life was spinning out of control. And there was nothing she could do about it.

The officers left and Nick reached out a hand and helped her to her feet. "Gather up what you're going to need to keep working."

She stuffed files and a portable hard drive into one section of her briefcase. "So, back to the hotel? Am I safe there?" She stared at him. "Is this guy crazy?"

"He could be. Or very crafty. Doing what he can to keep you on edge."

She shook her head slowly. "What else is he going to do?"

"Whatever he can to disrupt your routine so he can isolate you. But he has to find you first. We'll stay at the hotel, unless he tracks you there. In the meantime a crew will repair and clean your house. Then Doug's security guy will install a high end security system."

She squared her shoulders. "I want to go to the house, see what I can salvage. I didn't check the bathroom or the rest of the drawers in the bedroom."

"I did. Every bottle of shampoo, every bit of makeup, destroyed in some way. Even the toothpaste was stomped on. Not even a handkerchief was left uncut."

She shuddered. "Will I be able to go home sometime soon?"

"We can't make that decision yet. Remember, you're the target. He's trying to rattle you enough so you make a mistake and he can kidnap you."

"I won't get careless and let him win." Not if she could help it.

"That's the right attitude. We can stop at a store so you can pick up more things to replace what he destroyed."

"Then return to a locked room in a hotel." Resignation rode her voice. She had no choice.

"Is there another way out of this building? So we can avoid the lobby?"

"Yes. There's a private elevator down to the executive parking garage. I've been authorized to use it for night meetings. For safety."

"Today there's a safety issue. I say we use it."

She unlocked her desk and picked up the key. "Let's go."

"Okay. Then we can go shopping. Buy more clothes and other things that you need. Take your mind off what's happening. I'm told women like to shop."

"Not me. I hate shopping. But I need enough to get me through a week or so."

Nick made a quick call and arranged for a police officer to accompany them to the department store. Then turned to her. "We'll catch him. In the meantime, we'll also keep doing what we have to do. Let's go."

She picked up her purse and briefcase and headed out the office door, Nick right behind her.

"I wish I knew if I'll have a job when this is over." *If I'm still alive.*

NICK SHUT the door of the hotel suite and turned the dead bolt. They were locked in for the rest of the day.

And the night.

A second night alone with Tricia at the hotel. At least the hotel suite was neutral territory and not her personal space.

Tricia, still traumatized, had stopped in front of the couch, shopping bags surrounding her. Looking defeated. He couldn't blame her. This entire week had been non-stop trouble for her.

They'd delayed coming back by shopping and having lunch. She'd surprised him by how much she'd bought. Including a bedspread for the bed, once the mutilated mattress is replaced. And other things she didn't need at the hotel. She hadn't wanted to come back to the hotel any more than he did. Room service was scheduled for 6:00. The rest of the afternoon stretched ahead of them.

"I forgot scissors to cut the tags off these clothes. My scissors are at the house." Even her voice sounded tired. She placed the first bag on the couch and pulled out a pair of dark brown slacks and a peach silk blouse.

He reached into the pocket of his slacks and produced a Swiss Army Knife. He opened it to reveal the tiny, sharp scissors, then handed it to her. Her startled look changed to a half-amused stare. She took the scissors and picked up the slacks. "I'm sure I've forgotten things I was too rattled to remember."

The next items out of the shopping bag were bras and panties in shades of blue and purple. No red. A slight flush on her cheeks betrayed her thoughts. But she didn't try to hide the underwear from him. He'd seen everything she'd bought at the store. He'd been at her side, or right outside the fitting room.

He tried to distract his mind from her underwear, and how it fit her curves.

Maybe conversation, that was not about the stalker.

He sat on a nearby chair. She glanced at him and kept snipping tags and folding clothes.

She carried an armload to the door of her bedroom. "I'll hang up this much." She disappeared from view. When she returned, she sat in the space she'd cleared of clothes and reached into the next shopping bag.

"You never married. Have you come close?" He blurted out the big question on his mind since he'd arrived.

"No. Not even close." Her tone was emphatic.

It stung.

"You never married either, did you?"

"No."

"Neither of us seem destined for happy ever after." She clutched the sweater she was holding to her chest. "I've figured out why I'm not marrying. Have you?"

He was immediately uncomfortable. *You're the only woman I ever wanted for happily ever after.* "The right person hasn't come along for me. But you decided not to marry because of the way your father treated your mother."

She shook her head. "No. That's not right. But I'll tell you this, I'm never going to let myself need a man like my mother needed my father. He let her down."

A chill flowed through Nick. She needed him for her safety. Nothing more. Once the guy was caught, she'd regain her normal life. Without him. And he'd leave for L.A. Why did it hurt so much?

She set the beige sweater down and picked up a green one. "When my father left my mother, she never recovered. She worshiped him and he treated her like she didn't matter. That's not what a marriage is supposed to be."

"He left you too."

She folded the sweater in her hands and placed it on the couch beside her. A soft shade of a lighter green that would go well with the fall of dark brown hair that framed her face. He mentally shook himself to stop the straying thoughts.

"He was never a loving father. I didn't miss him as much as

my mother did. At least he sent money after he left, enough for us to live comfortably. My mother worked too. I doubt she could depend on money from my father, but she didn't discuss finances with me."

She frowned in a way that reminded Nick of someone trying to conjure up a memory and coming up with something they didn't like.

"What hurt me the most was the way my mother withdrew emotionally. Like she was incapable of love and affection. No hugs, no kisses. I was young. I needed those things."

"Abandoned by both your parents. No wonder you're so independent." He let his own memories sift into his conscious-ness. "My father passed on to me the legacy of the cop's life. He was a model cop, the so-called pillar of the community. He wanted justice, getting the bad guys. So do I." He said the words with the conviction he felt.

She set down the slacks in her hands. "Tell me again why you're not working as a cop in Los Angeles. Why you're here babysitting me." She challenged him with words and a don't-lie-to-me look.

"Legitimate question." He'd already given her the watered-down version. "The drug bust we were on developed into a gun battle and my partner was killed. I shot two men to save myself and the other two officers with me. I'm on administrative leave while they investigate. The lieutenant thinks I'm trigger happy. He'll find out I had no choice. They'll call me back to work when the inquiry wraps up."

"And how long will the inquiry take?"

"I honestly have no idea. But I won't leave you unprotected. I promise." A promise he'd keep, no matter what.

She hesitated. "So what kind of cop are you? The pillar of

the community or one of the wild ones who get the job done any way they can?"

He laughed. "I'm not my father." Then he grimaced. "He'd have been the first to come down on me hard. But I get results. The bad guys haven't killed me while I've been doing the job I was hired to do."

Though they'd tried. But so far he'd been able to avoid getting shot. And killed. "I don't think my actions caused the problems that night. We may have misread the situation going in."

"Is that what you think?"

"The plan was a good one. But it didn't work. The situation was different from what we'd expected. Maybe because the gang had inside information."

"You like your work." A statement, not a question.

"I do. I made the right choice, going to Los Angeles, taking the job offer, becoming a cop."

"And I made the right choice for me. Law school. This job." Her gaze held his.

But the chemistry between them had never gone away. Ten years. She had sailed past his defenses as if they were invisible.

CHAPTER 12

*R*oom service arrived on time. Tricia picked at the grilled chicken breast and roasted vegetables on her plate, eating very little. Then she reached for the gooey chocolate brownie with ice cream and chocolate syrup Nick had ordered for her. And took a big bite, making sure she included a gob of molten chocolate. He must have remembered her cravings for comfort food when she was upset. Ten years and he hadn't forgotten.

He was watching her and smiling. Three days in his company and she was far too comfortable having him around. Like the past ten years hadn't mattered. Was she starting to fall in love with him? Had she been in love with him when they were in college and didn't realize it? He had a depth she'd never seen when he was younger. She liked the new Nick very much. Too much.

She took another bite of the gooey chocolate and the flavor exploded on her tongue. She'd rather have the taste of Nick's kisses, but she couldn't let anything get started between them. Not when she was so vulnerable. But the comfort of his arms around her, last night and this morning... She wanted more.

The almost kiss the first night at her house would have to suffice. She knew he cared. Deep down inside it mattered that he cared. Yet a certain level of panic accompanied the satisfied feelings.

She glanced at him. Those dark eyes of his always betrayed what he was thinking. The smoldering depths were a giveaway. "I need to finish with the clothes I bought and get everything organized." She fled to the bedroom.

She bent over the bed to sort the stacks of clothes. A prickly feeling teased the nape of her neck. She wasn't alone. She slowly pivoted. Nick lounged against the door jamb.

"We forgot a suitcase so I can take the things I bought back to my house." She placed the filmy nightgown in the drawer and wished she'd bought cotton flannel pajamas instead. Since she was sharing space with Nick.

"We can get one tomorrow, then go see Doug. He said he'd be in his office."

She closed the drawer. "I'm going to bed early. I didn't get much sleep last night. Please shut the door."

He came forward instead, stopping in front of her. "Are you okay? You seem so uptight. Let me hold you." He reached out.

"Is that a good idea?" It wasn't. Yet she couldn't shove him out the door. Not when she craved his closeness.

She settled into his arms. She didn't have the strength to resist the offer of comfort.

"Relax. Let go of the tension."

She relaxed into his grasp. Burrowed into his chest, feeling the warmth of his body through their clothes. He caressed her back, her arms, until she melted into him.

Then she made the mistake of gazing up at him. At his mouth merely inches from hers.

Then she couldn't say who moved first. His lips touched hers and lit a fire deep inside her, that intensified way beyond mere comfort. The embers flared into flames and she succumbed to the sensations, to the sheer bliss of being held by him, kissed by him.

He tasted of coffee and pure masculinity. He tightened his grasp, then his mouth became possessive, in the way that was pure Nick. He plundered her mouth and ripples of desire coursed through her, closing off her rational mind. Nick was what she wanted. She lost herself in the thrill of the kiss, of his hands, of his body heat, of the safety of his arms.

How could things escalate this fast between them? They hadn't seen each other in over ten years. She felt the kiss clear down to her toes and everywhere in between. Then he shifted his hold on her, breathing heavily.

"I'm sorry. That wasn't a good idea." His voice was hoarse with need.

She pushed out of his arms, her body tingling. She'd lost control. She was as much to blame as he was. She gazed at him as she slowly regained some of that control.

"I should have stayed out of here." He left the room, closing the door behind him.

In a daze, she touched her still-tingling lips and stared at the door. How could she possibly sleep?

NICK TRIED to act casual through their room service breakfast and getting ready to go see Doug. But that kiss hung between them. Tricia was quiet and subdued. Not talking any more than she had to. Not meeting his gaze any more than she had to. Not getting any closer to him than she had to.

She remained quiet when they took the elevator down to the parking garage and got into the SUV for the drive to the agency.

"Call Doug. Tell him we're on the way." He tossed Tricia his phone. She made the call, then handed him the phone without touching him.

They rounded the corner onto the tree-lined street where the office was located. Doug stood on the steps of the brick-faced building, leaning on his cane, a pretty blond at his side. One of his employees?

Or a friend? Patti had been dead for five years. Nick parked in front of the building and they got out of the car.

Doug greeted them and introduced Alison Steele, crushing Nick's momentary fantasy.

"Glad you're back from Los Angeles." Nick extended his hand.

"Thanks. I was a little scared down there. Things have changed since I've been up here, even though the area is familiar." Her grip was firm.

"The drug wars have changed the city." He frowned. "My job keeps me out on those mean streets."

Her expression was one of contentment that said she was happy to be here in Portland. He couldn't help wondering if Doug himself was at least part of it. He could hope. But he also wondered why she spent three days driving from L.A. to Portland. The trip was possible in two days, with a stop to sleep. But Doug had said she was on vacation. So she took her time. Nick could relate.

"I have a new vehicle for you." Doug gestured toward the parking lot at the side of the building. "The guy has seen the

SUV. Take the silver Beemer in the first space. The tinted windows ought to help. At least he won't be able to see Tricia from some angles."

Nick and Tricia followed Doug and Alison inside and down the hall to Doug's office. He sat behind his desk. Alison stayed by the door. Nick and Tricia took the chairs in front of the desk.

"Anything else, Doug, before I go home to freshen up?" Alison's voice had a nice lilt to it. She could easily be mistaken for an office worker rather than the accomplished PI sharp-shooter she was.

"You don't need to come back. Everything else can wait until Monday." Doug's dismissive wave accompanied a genuine smile. "See you then."

Nick stood to catch her attention. "I'm curious about something. Velasquez told me Moreno tied you to Doug and put you on his hit list. How did he figure it out?"

"Dumb luck. Someone I'd known since high school had joined up with him and knew I'd come to Portland, that I was working for the agency. I grew up in south central L.A."

"We'll be protecting each other." Doug grinned widely. Like he fully accepted the situation. Interesting.

"I'll see you Monday." Alison left and Nick sat down.

Doug watched her go out the door. Then snapped his attention back to them. "Chet Richardson called earlier. He's been interviewing people. We've gone beyond database searches and the footwork has begun. He seems to be zeroing in on Jasper, who has admitted he has a set of Tricia's keys."

"I had completely forgotten about the keys. I should have changed the locks after I broke up with him." Tricia gripped her hands tightly in her lap.

"Don't worry." Doug gazed at her, as if assessing her state of mind. "He'll be checked out thoroughly. And Chet wants to talk to both of you this morning, to make sure you don't have information that he doesn't." He glanced at the clock on his desk. "He'll be here in about ten minutes."

"Better than the hotel," Tricia said. "The fewer people who know our location, the safer I am. I don't go back to my house, do I?"

"No you don't." Relief flooded through Nick. She'd made the decision herself and he wouldn't have to play the heavy. The hotel suite would have to do. As long as the guy didn't find them.

Tricia sank back in her chair. He studied her solemn expression. She regretted that kiss last night. But they'd have to stay in that hotel suite and remain in close quarters. Until the guy was caught. Or until he found them.

CHAPTER 13

 ricia settled into the passenger seat of the Beemer and fastened her seat belt. "I don't want to go back to the hotel." She sounded as pouty and rebellious as a teenager, but she didn't care.

Nick frowned. "You agreed that the hotel room was the safest place."

"We're in a different car." A sleek silver car that begged to be driven somewhere interesting. At the hotel she'd be locked in the room. With Nick.

He gazed at her a moment, then started the car and drove out of the agency parking lot. "Do you want to do more shopping?"

"No. It's Saturday. I'm not working. I want to do something I don't usually do. I want to get away from town. Away from responsibilities." She'd surprised herself with that announcement. When had she last done something that didn't have a specific purpose?

Nick coasted to a stop at a traffic light and his wide-eyed

stare in her direction told her she'd surprised him too. "I repeat, the hotel room is the safest place for you."

"I don't feel safe there. I feel like I'm being punished for being a woman, for being vulnerable."

"We'll catch him. Be patient. Give us more time." Exasperation leaked into his tone.

"I'm out of patience. My stalker is free to go where he wants." Panic crept into her voice. "I've lost my privacy. I've lost my freedom. I've lost my feeling of security."

"I know." He said the words quietly but with a power that made her heart swell. He did care.

"Are you sorry you're here guarding me?" She tamped down the panic.

"No."

He didn't hesitate. That was a good sign. How far could she push him today? "Let's go for a drive. Out of town. He won't be anywhere near us."

"Unless he's following us." Nick clicked on his turn signal and swerved right. Then checked the rear-view mirror. He made three more circuits around the block, then drove into a residential neighborhood.

"If he's tailing us, he's smarter than I am." He turned onto a busy street.

Apprehension, but also exhilaration, flooded through her. "We switched cars. You're with me. He won't do anything."

"I hope I don't regret this." Nick words carried an undertone of uneasiness. He changed lanes and took the on ramp to the freeway.

After several more freeway changes and forty minutes, they left the city behind.

Once they reached an area of open highway, Tricia nestled against the back of the seat. "Thanks. If something goes wrong,

I'll take the blame." She ignored the guilty feelings that arose and tried to relax.

"I'm shirking my duties as a bodyguard. I should have taken you straight to the hotel."

She ignored his grim words. "Where are we going?" She glanced to the left of the highway, at the Columbia River stretched like a dull green ribbon under a gray sky.

"Are you nervous?"

"No. Not really." She squirmed in the seat. "I'm not sure what I want anymore."

He glanced her way, then back to the highway. "How about Multnomah Falls? I haven't been there in years."

"Good choice. I haven't been there for a while." She focused on the river. She liked water, especially the ocean or big rivers, like the Columbia. And waterfalls.

"I shouldn't have let you talk me into this." He sounded as if he were already regretting his decision.

"What could possibly happen that hasn't already?" The familiar cold chill rocketed down her spine and she shivered. And almost told him to turn around.

"He could grab you. Whatever we do is risky. He's not going to disappear."

"I'm willing to take a chance." Today she felt a little bit brave.

"We could get rained on."

He'd changed the subject. He was driving east, and he'd stopped arguing. Her mood lightened. "I don't mind the rain. It's comforting in a way. Sometimes rain makes me want to pull inside and hide. Not today. Today I can hide in the rain."

"Why would you want to hide? You're a career woman with so much going for you." His tone indicated skepticism.

"I'm not as sure of myself as I like to let people think."

"Could have fooled me."

"I did, for a while. A long time ago."

He didn't say anything. Was bringing up the past a huge mistake?

To avoid more personal conversation, she gazed out the window, aware of the miles slipping by. She ignored the too-close Nick and alternated her focus from the white-capped, wind-whipped waves of the Columbia River on one side of the highway to the massive basalt-studded cliffs on the other side. And the occasional small waterfall.

Nick took the freeway off ramp to the parking lot at the falls and she got out of the Beemer onto the asphalt pavement, giving up the limited protection of the tinted windows. Panic built inside her until she took a deep breath to calm herself. She needed this time outside the confines of the hotel room.

Nick's eyes narrowed, his brows furrowed. "Are you okay?"

"Yes. I'm glad we came." The roar of the double falls in the distance caught her attention. The sight of the cascading water tumbling down the cliff was magical. She'd never get tired of looking at it.

She shivered. A brisk breeze had chilled her cheeks and her arms. She reached into the backseat of the car, grabbed her jacket, and put it on. Nick had done the same. She shut the car door and inhaled the scent of the rain approaching, along with the fragrance of the gigantic Douglas firs dotting the landscape. Then the acrid odor of diesel exhaust from a truck pulling out of the parking lot mingled with the fresh scents.

Nick at her side, she hurried toward the pedestrian tunnel under the highway. The rumbling of the vehicles passing over them on the freeway echoed off the concrete walls.

She climbed the stone steps, careful of her footing, then paused in the public area below the falls. Leaves drifted down from the oak trees as the breeze tugged them loose. She brushed a golden leaf off her jacket. A few people milled around despite the wind and threatening clouds.

The fine mist from the stream of cascading water drifted over them. "We've had plenty of rain lately. The creeks in the hills are running fast and deep."

"I love watching the water," Nick said. "So much power."

"Especially when so much comes down at once." She breathed in the misty air and felt the first drops of rain. "I'm hungry. Let's eat lunch at the lodge. Maybe this is only a shower and won't last long."

"Okay. Food first. Then we check out the falls from the bridge."

With the majestic roar of the falls echoing in the canyon, they headed toward the restaurant.

Their table sat next to the windows and the view of the trees outside. The dull light of the rainy day shone through the many window panes and skylights. After the waitress took their order, Nick leaned back in his chair with a questioning look that was also a half frown.

"You said something in the car that has me wondering, about having fooled me. About your feelings for me? About our relationship? About a future for us?"

Her heart seized. "I'm sorry I brought up the subject." She never should have admitted the truth. She'd become too comfortable with Nick. Not a good sign.

"I'm glad you did. I have questions. I've had years to analyze what went wrong, I can't come up with an answer to why you ran scared."

"You think I ran scared because of you?" She tried for a light, teasing tone.

"At the time, I did. I thought you were afraid of a serious

relationship. That what you wanted was casual sex with no strings attached."

"Nick! That's crude. We had much more, or we wouldn't have been together for those two years." So much more that it had scared her. Not something she would admit, though.

She had been perilously close to giving up her dream of law school. For him. A flare of inner longing warned her the conversation had strayed into a topic too dangerous to discuss. She twisted her hands in front of her. "My mother taught me not to trust men."

"I'm not your father. I wouldn't have let you down."

"But you weren't talking marriage. You wanted me to move in with you while you achieved your dream of becoming a cop. I had dreams too. And a scholarship to law school."

His crooked smile was half grimace. "I was rather callous, wasn't I?"

"More like selfish. You wanted me to trust you but you weren't offering me the security of marriage."

"Your mother's marriage hadn't been secure. Your father left when you were ten and never returned." He said the words tentatively, like he was afraid she'd take offense.

She twisted in the seat. "Maybe I was scared I'd be hurt, like my father hurt my mother. So I hurt you instead. Maybe I wasn't ready for permanent. Maybe I won't ever be ready." She braced for his reaction.

He stared at her for a full minute. As if making up his mind about something. "I wanted permanent then, but didn't realize it. I've lived alone for a long time. I'm not sure permanent is what I want."

"Then we don't have a problem." The words tumbled out.

"Yes, we do." His words were emphatic, accompanied by a

gaze that oozed pure heat. Waves of desire coursed through her. Along with alarm bells.

The waitress appeared with their sandwiches. Tricia bit into hers and tried to ignore him. If she were chewing, she couldn't continue what had become an uncomfortable subject. What was going to happen? They were sharing a suite. Two bedrooms next to each other. Nothing would stop them from sharing one bed.

Is that what she wanted? The truth? No, because it would be only sex. It wouldn't lead to anything remotely resembling a relationship. She had her job here in Portland. His job was a good thousand miles away, down in Los Angeles.

He slowly chewed the bite in his mouth while keeping his gaze locked with hers.

She took a few more bites, the tension inside building, till the roasted turkey and bacon on whole wheat no longer tasted good. She shoved the plate aside and stared out the window at the breeze whipping the golden leaves off the elms and the oaks.

Nick finished his lunch and pushed his plate away. "Let's go out. The rain has stopped, at least temporarily."

Nick paid the bill and they pushed through the door to the outside. "No rain. Let's go up to the falls."

He held out his hand and she took it as if it was a normal thing to do. They turned to the right and accessed the trail to the bridge. From there they'd have a better view of the cascading water.

At the top of the trail, Tricia stepped onto the concrete bridge. An impressive wall of water pummeled down the mountainside and into the pool below. A dizzy, head-spinning sensation threw her off balance and she stumbled. Nick steadied her, then pulled her against him.

"I'm sorry. I have a problem with heights." She clung to him. "Even looking up at something high or looking down a long distance. I'm a wimp."

"It's not a weakness. Merely something some people live with." No one else was on the bridge. He nuzzled her ear, and a feathery kiss on her neck sent a shiver of delight through her. He tightened his grip on her.

She gazed at him, at the intensity of those dark brown eyes, before he brought his mouth down on hers and she closed her eyes to savor the moment. And lose herself in the heat of his kiss. Her body responded with that inner flame that turned her insides to molten liquid. Had he not been holding her, she would have melted into a puddle at his feet.

For long moments she was lost in his embrace, not caring about anything but the sensations that sparked through her body. Yet another thought wiggled into her consciousness. Kissing him was making her want so much more. More than she could have.

When he broke the kiss, at the periphery of her vision, she saw someone down below with a camera aimed their way. "That guy. Is he taking our picture?" She spun around and pointed down.

He looked where she pointed. "Let's go. I want to keep that dude in our sights. The hood he's wearing hides his face." The note of alarm in his voice triggered a spiral of fear down her spine.

He grasped her arm and they jogged down the trail, dodging several people coming up. Her heart pounded in rhythm with their strides.

The guy with the camera broke into a run, sprinting for the tunnel. Knocking over a little boy in his path.

Tricia's heart rate sped up. When they got to level ground,

they ran as fast as they could. Through the tunnel and into the parking lot. No sign of the guy with the camera.

"I think we just saw your stalker." Anger laced Nick's words.

Tricia shivered, and not from the cold. "I thought we weren't followed."

"I didn't think we were. This guy is cunning. And dangerous."

CHAPTER 14

*N*ick glanced at the empty hallway. Then shut the hotel room door and flipped the dead bolt.

Tricia walked straight to her bedroom door, then turned. Her purse dangled from her fingers. Her eyes had a far-off stare.

"You're safe in here." He kept his tone positive.

"No, I'm not. Wherever I am, I'm in danger." Her voice shook, a slight tremor laced with anger.

She wheeled around and into the bedroom, calling out to him. "I'm going to stay in here a while. I want to be alone." Her bedroom door snapped shut behind her.

Guilt coiled inside him. She was spooked and he didn't blame her. He shouldn't have taken her out of town. He shouldn't have kissed her. He shouldn't have let his needs interfere with his judgment. He was positive the guy hadn't followed them. But somehow he'd found out where they were going. A breakdown in security.

He'd have to tell Doug. He checked his cell phone. Three text messages from Doug. Each one angrier than the last. That coil of guilt tightened into a throbbing knot. He punched in Doug's number.

Doug answered immediately. "Open the door. I just stepped out of the elevator into the hall." His voice held a clipped, angry tone.

Sweat popped out on Nick's brow. He hurried to the door, unlocked it, and held it open.

Doug brushed by him, limping, leaning on his cane. "I thought I could trust you. Why didn't you answer your phone or my texts?" He lifted the cane and poked the air.

Nick's throat constricted. "We drove out to Multnomah Falls and got back a few minutes ago. We must have been out of cell range." He forced out the words, trying for an even-keeled tone to diffuse at least part of Doug's anger. Before admitting the stalker found them.

"Where's Tricia?"

"She shut herself in the bedroom." He pointed toward the closed door.

"Good. I want to talk to you. When you didn't answer, you gave me a scare." Words still laced with anger.

Nick's coil of guilt tightened. He'd let Doug down. "Sorry. I didn't think about you worrying."

"You should have." Doug dropped into a chair, stretched out his legs, and put the cane on the floor.

Nick tried for a conciliatory tone. "Tricia wanted to stay out of the hotel for a while. I was concerned about her. She says she feels like a prisoner."

"She's under our protection. We're responsible for her safety." Again, clipped and emphatic.

"Right."

"Stay objective. If you can't, I'll pull you and find someone else to put with her."

"Point taken. I'm doing a job, even if it's with someone I cared far too much about years ago." Nick walked to the bedroom door and listened. Water was running in the tub.

"You're both reacting like your relationship was serious," Doug said.

"I guess neither of us realized how deep our feelings were. But that was a long time ago."

"Tricia's a victim. You're a professional. A detective. A body-guard. Someone with a job to do." Pure Doug speech. He was in commander-in-chief mode.

Nick sat on the couch. Confession time. "We have a problem. The stalker found us. He was wearing a hooded sweatshirt and took a picture of us from long range."

Doug sat up straight in the chair. "You're positive it was him?"

"When we started after him, he ran through the tunnel."

"He followed you out there. You got careless." Doug's eyes were focused and intent.

"No. He was not behind us when we left your office. I didn't have a tail. I made sure."

"Which means he was watching the office and saw me tell you to drive the Beemer." He shifted in the chair. "The car's probably bugged."

"If it is, he can track us to this hotel. The car's in the under-ground garage." Nick gestured toward the floor.

"I'll send Rafe to check out the car for a hidden GPS. He was out of town for a couple of weeks."

"Good idea."

"This guy is smart. Stay alert. Don't let anything distract you."

Doug's hidden message. Don't let his feelings for Tricia get in the way of protecting her.

"Do we sit tight until someone IDs him or he does something that gives himself away?" Nick crossed to the window. The roof of the building next door was at least five stories above their room level. The blinds were drawn on the windows opposite and an alley separated the two buildings. No threat from there.

"If your location has been compromised, you'll be moving tomorrow. Stay in the room tonight. Order room service."

"Okay." He returned to the couch.

"One other matter," Doug said. "Chet's been interviewing the men on Tricia's list. Andy Pederson and Rob Jasper have said things that should be checked out."

"And Jasper has keys to the old locks." The thought bothered Nick.

"Both men care too much about Tricia and would go out with her again if she'd see them."

"I thought Jasper was married."

"And divorced. He said he hadn't contacted Tricia, but was planning to. Andy approached her Wednesday morning and she refused to go to lunch with him. I want you to interview both of them, for another perspective."

"I can talk to them tomorrow, unless we have to move. But what about Tricia?"

"I'll send someone to stay with her. Not me. The guy may have figured out that we're related." He grimaced, a pained expression. "He could have followed me this afternoon. And discovered you're on the fifth floor."

"We'll take complete precautions."

He picked up his cane, then stood. His scrunched-brow stare meant there was more.

"What? What else do you want to say?"

"Take care of her and don't do anything to jeopardize her safety."

"I won't. Call me when you've made the arrangements for tomorrow."

"And I'll tell you if Rafe finds a bug on the car." He let himself out the door.

Nick flipped the dead bolt. Doug was worried about him becoming emotionally involved with Tricia. Hell. Too late. He'd never gotten over her. No way out, except to finish the job and scoot back to L.A. Before he self-destructed.

TRICIA LISTENED by the bedroom door. The outer door clicked shut. Then silence. Doug had left.

She dreaded facing Nick, but at least she'd avoided Doug. What had begun as a welcome break this morning had ended in disaster.

Entirely her fault. Because she wanted to stay away from the hotel. She glanced around the room. The walls were closing in on her. A prisoner. That's what she had said earlier. She was a prisoner because of her vulnerability. Not fair.

She slipped out of the hotel bathrobe, annoyed with herself for forgetting to buy a bathrobe yesterday, among other things. She wasn't usually this disorganized.

Then she picked out a soft beige lounging suit from a drawer in the dresser, and put it on. The fabric was smooth and soothing against her skin. The outfit covered her and fit loosely. Another barrier.

She opened the door. Nick had turned on the TV news and was sprawled on the couch.

He glanced up. "I'm hungry. What do you want from room service?"

Was that guilt she saw in his eyes? She hadn't heard what Doug said, but she could imagine. She hadn't listened to Nick so he got the blame. Guilt soared through her. "Nothing. I'm not hungry."

"It's a long time till breakfast. And you didn't eat all of your lunch." The look he sent her way was half smile, half question. "I'm getting a steak. They have salads too."

Her immediate reaction was to stubbornly cling to her refusal of food. But starving herself wouldn't get her out of here any faster. "Okay. Order me a Cobb."

He called in their order on the hotel phone.

Letting Nick into her house, then sharing this suite with him, was the closest she'd come to living with a guy. She'd always resisted giving up her freedom and independence. So she pushed men away. Including Nick. Especially Nick. Because she was most vulnerable to him and the passion he awakened in her.

She sat in a chair and Nick returned to the couch.

"I'm sorry I got you into trouble with Doug."

"I'm the one who messed up. I wasn't doing my job."

"Why did Doug show up here?"

"He tried to call us and text, but we were out of range of a cell tower. He was worried. And angry."

"So what happens next?"

"He's having Rafe check out the car, looking for a bug. We may have to change hotels."

"He could find us here tonight?" She didn't try to disguise the fear in her voice.

"Maybe."

"Hiding is making me crazy." The tension in her body increased, with the hint of a headache in her left temple. The dull ache signaled more pain to come. Maybe from lack of food. He was right. She hadn't eaten much of her lunch, when the conversation had become too personal. Nick had that effect on her.

She tried with difficulty to concentrate on the evening news instead of Nick. He took up far too much space in the room, in her mind, in her heart. She'd keep her guard up. She did not want to need Nick for more than protection.

When room service knocked, Nick motioned her into the bedroom. After the server left, he opened the door for her.

"Was that necessary?" Her voice held a sharp edge.

"Yes. We don't take any more chances."

Nick's cell phone rang. He answered. And his side of the conversation said he didn't like what he heard. He ended the call.

"The car was bugged. He can trace us to this hotel."

"But maybe not the room we're in."

"We can't count on that. What if he followed Doug? We'll move in the morning, and tonight we stay alert for anything out of the ordinary."

"Shouldn't we go to a different hotel tonight?"

"No, not till morning. Let's eat. Clean up as much as we can. The table stays in the room for the night too."

Cold reality set in. No matter where she was, she was in danger.

～

NICK SHIFTED ON THE COUCH, taking a break from the file he was reading. Tricia was bent over her laptop, concentrating, trying to work, despite the interruptions. Her boss had called two hours earlier to check on her progress. He wanted answers to the financial problem as soon as possible. Tension lines were visible on her face.

The fire alarm screeched. Nick's stomach knotted. He bolted from the couch.

Tricia jumped up. "Do you think it's a fire, or a false alarm? What if he's out in the hall?"

"We stay here until I know what's going on. He could grab you in the confusion if we leave the room." He picked up the hotel phone and called the switchboard. The message from the operator said to evacuate immediately. "Let me speak to the manager. Police business. This is Detective Nick Castellani."

Two minutes passed, then, "This is the manager. Why aren't you evacuating?"

"Because I want to know first where the fire is located. I have a good reason for asking the question. Police business."

"The fire is in the stairwell on the second floor. And should be out shortly. It hasn't spread."

"Thank you." He hung up the phone. "Fire set in a stairwell. I've blown our cover to get the information. The guy should leave when he figures out his plan didn't work. This place will be swarming with cops."

"Nick, I'm scared." She hugged her body with her arms.

"He's not getting to you. I promise."

He grabbed his cell phone to call Doug. Doug answered immediately.

"The fire alarm was set off in the hotel. I think our boy set a fire in the stairwell. To get the information, I blew our cover."

"That doubles the bad news. I was about to call you. Chet got the DNA report on the cigarette butts."

"Nothing helpful?"

"Distressing is more like it. Our suspect is a man who's killed at least twice. The FBI is fully involved and expediting the DNA tests, checking for more matches."

"Whoa! Repeat that."

Tricia moved to his side, obviously wanting to hear what Doug said. He relayed the information to her and she sank into a chair, her eyes wide.

He quickly assessed their situation. "I think we're safe for the night, with firemen and police swarming the hotel."

"I'll have another place for you by morning and another vehicle with a driver."

"Make it someone the guy won't recognize."

"Erik doesn't get out much. No one sees him unless they have technical needs. I'll send him. How's Tricia holding up?"

"She's nervous and scared." She was clutching a sofa pillow in front of her, squeezing it.

"Stay inside the room until Erik gets there and calls you. I'll send him early. Don't order room service breakfast. You'll stop for breakfast on the way."

"Okay."

"Tomorrow you go to a safe house that will be stocked with food and anything else you'll need. Tricia won't be going to work on Monday."

"I'll tell her the change of plans. Thanks, Doug."

"Stay alert." He ended the call.

Tricia's wide-eyed stare said she didn't like what she'd heard.

"We go to a safe house tomorrow."

"He's really a killer?" Her tone was questioning, as if she couldn't quite believe it yet.

"Two DNA matches to those cigarette butts. Same man. Your stalker is definitely a killer."

He'd heard the cliches about color draining from a face, but for the first time he witnessed the phenomenon. Tricia's face was beyond pale.

CHAPTER 15

*T*he Hummer crawled along the narrow rutted lane through a canopy of thick Douglas fir. Nick peered through the dense foliage, making out a structure in the distance.

"A log cabin?" Tricia's voice held a note of dismay.

Erik drove around a bend in the road, broke free of the forest, and stopped in front of the house.

Not a log cabin. A massive two-story log house nestled among more large trees that closed in around it like a protective shield.

Nick opened the passenger door and gazed at the trees, the house, the utter seclusion. "This'll do."

Tricia got out of the vehicle. "It's like being in a cage. Those trees surround the house like a high fence. I had no idea Uncle Doug owned such a place."

Her tone was laced with anger. Did she resent not knowing? Or resented having to hide out here?

"It's Doug's private getaway destination, but he bought it

also to use as a safe house if he ever needed one." Erik opened his door and got out. "You're the first ones to get to use it." His half smile was directed at Tricia. "Since your hotel room was compromised, this is the safest place for you."

"Uncle Doug wants to keep me securely locked up." Definitely a note of anger in her voice.

Erik closed the Hummer door. "Because our suspect has killed at least twice. And there could be more victims."

Fear and defiance flashed in Tricia's eyes. And more of that anger. Could they keep Tricia locked up for a long time and hope the guy leaves town? Not likely. Nick had an uneasiness he couldn't shake. Coming out here could prove to be the wrong thing to do. Only postponing the inevitable showdown.

"There's another SUV in the garage," Erik said. "In case you need to get out fast. The keys are on a pegboard in the kitchen. Otherwise, you stay here and someone will bring you more food when you need it."

"I hope Doug and the police have a plan to identify the guy and end this standoff." Nick led the way up the steps to the cedar plank porch running along the front of the house. Tricia clutched her purse and briefcase, saying nothing.

"This place is a fortress." Erik unlocked the massive deadbolt on the door. "Surveillance cameras are mounted on the outside, and are tied in with a sophisticated alarm system that's wired into a local agency."

Nick glanced up. One camera pointed directly at them.

"Wait until I disarm the system." Erik hurried inside. He reappeared in a few moments. "Alarm is off. I'll give you the security code before I leave."

Erik helped with the luggage, then showed them the keypad and had them memorize the security code. He told Nick to call

Doug as soon as they were settled. When he'd left, Nick surveyed the interior of the house.

Tricia approached the table in the dining room. A vase of fresh red rosebuds sat in the middle of the table. "Doug knows I love red roses. Is this bouquet a peace offering, because I don't want to hide out?"

He smiled. "Could be." Typical Doug behavior.

"This is no little cabin." Tricia whirled around, taking in the entire great room.

"A rich man's vacation home. Secluded, luxurious, a perfect hideaway."

"If one wants to hide." More anger in Tricia's tone. She picked up her two bags and headed down the hallway and up the staircase. Within ten minutes, she'd returned downstairs, took her laptop out of her briefcase, and sat in a plush chair in the corner, by a small table.

Nick had put his luggage in another bedroom and come downstairs with his own laptop and briefcase. He sat on the leather sectional that separated the dining area from the living room. Two huge windows looked out on the patio and flower garden. Beyond the small garden the tall fir trees formed a barrier at the edge of the forest.

He could see why Tricia had a closed-in feeling.

"Erik told me to call Doug." He took his cell phone out of his pocket. "No service here."

"My boss won't be able to call me." Her voice held panic.

He spotted a phone on the end table, and scooted over. He picked up the handset, then punched in the number for Doug's private line.

"I was waiting for your call," Doug said. "Chet sent preliminary information this morning to pass on to you. This is one sadistic dude. You're not going to like what you see in the file."

"I suspected as much."

"I'm faxing the file to you instead of using email. You'll see why. My study, and the fax machine, is off the hallway, second door on the left." His tone was grim.

Nick braced for more bad news. "And this file is going to tell us who this guy is?"

"No name. But a record of what he's done for the past four years. We have DNA matches to six brutal rapes and murders. We're dealing with a psychopath."

"How can we be sure it's our guy?"

"Chet found a neighbor who saw a man in a hooded sweatshirt standing at the corner of Tricia's yard, smoking those cigarettes."

"That fits the information we have so far." Nick's gut tightened. Tricia was watching him intently. "How much do I share?"

"Don't tell Tricia anything you think she can't handle."

"Okay."

Tricia's eyes narrowed. Of course she'd want all the information. He expected that from her.

"I'll talk to you later, after you've had a chance to read the file," Doug said. "I've kept back five pages with gory details I definitely don't want her to see. You'll understand when I show you." He ended the call.

"Okay, spill it." Tricia's hands were on her hips and a scowl wrinkled her brow. He could imagine the kinds of information Doug wasn't sending.

"A fax is coming through." He headed for the study. Tricia followed. He opened the door and saw the pages collecting in the tray.

"I'm going to read the file too. You're not hiding anything from me."

"Are you sure you want all the details? This guy is a monster."

"Yes." Hot anger blazed in her eyes. "I'm not a delicate little girl you have to shield from the truth."

He couldn't blame her. The guy had targeted her. But both he and Doug were well aware of the thoroughness of police files. He hoped what Doug sent wasn't too graphic.

WHEN THE MACHINE SHUT OFF, Nick picked up the pile of pages. Tricia followed him to the living room, not letting those pages out of her sight. He wasn't going to hide anything from her. Her life was the one threatened.

They settled on the couch, side by side.

Nick picked up the first page and began reading. And stopped. "Six DNA matches to six victims of rape and murder over the past four years." He said it slowly, his words pulsing with anger.

A crushing pressure constricted her chest. "Six previous victims." Her voice shook.

"Four years, six cities, six murders. Our suspect killed them. No mistake. Too many details match, as well as the DNA." He waved the page in the air. "The DNA of this killer was on those cigarette butts found outside your house."

A deep chill climbed her spine and radiated throughout her body. She grasped her arms in front of her chest and closed her eyes.

"You okay?"

"No."

He reached for her, settling her against his side. She felt his warmth, his caring. And opened her eyes. "Go on. What else?" Her voice still shook.

Nick cleared his throat, as if he didn't want to continue. "In each case he'd terrorized his victim, invaded her home, stolen underwear and jewelry." He drew back. "They were found wearing nothing but the jewelry."

She cringed. "That's why he took the pearls and the bracelet." She wiggled out of his arms. "How did they die?" She'd let him tell her. If she did read that whole file, she'd have nightmares.

"They bled to death. The photos are here too."

The chill increased, setting off a shaking sensation in her shoulders, her arms, her legs. "I don't want to see the photos. Tell me what I need to know." Her words came out as a whisper. She was falling into a deep dark pit of despair.

"Every one of the women was a career woman. Single, in her thirties, living alone." Nick's voice sounded far away. Unreal.

"A life like mine." Her imagination conjured up an image, her naked and bleeding, wearing the pearls and the diamond bracelet. "I don't want to die like they did."

She stood and walked to the window, and stared at the tall fir trees across the back of the garden. Those trees that formed a tight line. A barricade.

What if he already knew where she was? Those trees wouldn't help. "He could be out there, waiting for darkness."

"The security system here is state of the art."

"And that's supposed to make me feel better about being locked up in this house? For how long?" She eased down into the corner of the couch. On the far end from Nick.

"Until we catch him."

She studied the serious expression on Nick's face. Frustration mingled with the fear inside her. "The way I see it, I have two choices. One is to stay in hiding for however many weeks or months it takes for the police and the FBI to figure out who the guy is. Lose my job, my income, probably my house." *And end up in bed with Nick.* The more time alone with him, the harder it would be to resist temptation.

"And two?"

"Go back to work to save my job. The FBI and the police will be working to figure out who the guy is. If I'm in town, he may do something suspicious."

"Too risky." His words were emphatic. And didn't surprise her.

"Your job is risky."

"I'm a cop. Goes with the job."

"Life is a risk. I have to keep working."

"You can work out here."

"How? Your cell phone didn't have service. Mine won't either. I can't use the land line, because the number can be traced. I need answers to questions. I need access to people who are in the office. So I'm stuck."

"Better stuck than dead."

Her chances of living a normal life seemed bleak before. Now those chances could be completely out of reach. Hiding out here in this safe house was a huge mistake. She was trapped.

CHAPTER 16

"*I* figured out how they manipulated the figures."

Nick glanced up from his laptop, from the report he'd downloaded while they were in Portland. Tricia's mouth was set in a grim line. "What did you find?"

She set her laptop on the coffee table. "My instincts were right when I scanned the stack of papers. I found a spreadsheet page that contains the missing bid. I remember that it was stuck to another page when I was quickly scanning the stack. And I see how they hid the truth by changing the formulas. I'm no spreadsheet genius, but I know something about the formulas and how to use them."

"What can you do about it?"

"I have ammunition. They didn't hide their tracks completely. Whoever it was." She picked up her coffee cup.

"Is there something you can do now?"

"I can show Talbot the bid did exist, that I hadn't doctored the figures. He's saying we never had enough money promised and I was covering up the deficit. He believed I was lying and that's why he's been threatening to fire me. He told me that if I can't save the project, my job is gone."

"You mean someone has deliberately hidden the truth from him and made you the scapegoat? No wonder you've been upset about the project." After seeing the grim expression on her face, he could better understand what was driving her to disregard her own safety.

"I have to go back to work. I can save my job. Unless Talbot is part of the scheme to place the blame on me."

"You're forgetting something. There's a killer out there who's after you. His objective is rape and your slow death."

She shuddered and her expression changed to one of defeat. She picked up the file Nick had left on the couch, and thumbed through it, stopping on a page describing the finding of one victim. She read part of the page, closed the file and flung it down. Her hunched shoulders reflected that defeat.

"I have to do something." She said the words quietly. He heard her easily. There were no other sounds in the room.

"I can't stay here, and lose everything I've worked for over the years. Without a good reference from Talbot Enterprises, I'll have trouble finding a new job. Besides, I feel like a prisoner out here. I want to return to town, go back to work. And see what happens."

"We've been over this before. You'd deliberately put yourself in danger to live what you term a normal life?"

"So I hide for possibly years? Until he's caught?" She stood and paced to the window and back, several times.

"You hide until we figure out who he is. I won't let that guy get his hands on you." He pointed at the file on the couch. "I don't want you to end up like those six women."

She settled into a chair near the huge stone fireplace that

dominated one wall. "I'll do whatever it takes to end this fiasco. It's been on my mind since we left the hotel."

The anger in her voice was like the anger he'd heard earlier. Now he understood why and it made sense. "We don't have the guy's identity. But we have the details that show us how dangerous he is."

"We can't figure out who he is until he does something suspicious. He may not find me here." She gazed around the room. "He'll wait. I can't hide here for the rest of my life." She almost shouted the words.

"I realize that."

She looked startled. "Then why are you trying to keep me here?"

"Hey, I'm not having fun either. This is not my usual line of work. And I don't have access to email or any details of the investigation unless I call Doug or Chet."

She gasped and stared at him. "I'm sorry. I've been so focused on my own misery, I wasn't thinking about you and what you've given up to protect me."

He was tempted to tell her the rest, that being around her and keeping his hands off her was the most difficult part of the job. But they shouldn't be discussing the chemistry between them. "I've been thinking too, of going on the offensive. Make him show his hand. But also keep you completely protected."

She rose from the chair. "I was by myself until a few days ago. Things have gotten worse since you've been with me. He's trying to scare you off. Make me get rid of you."

"So he can kidnap you. Remember, he's been inside your house twice. He's intelligent and skillful."

She paced to the window again, keeping her back to him. "Maybe he's not smart enough to figure out that we're setting a trap for him."

Nick grimaced. "He's smart, for a criminal. No one saw him slash the desk or slap the paint on your front door. The police questioned people who were at both places. And checked the surveillance tapes. Nothing. The camera in the hallway near your office door had black tape over it."

She slowly pivoted, hands on her hips. "Which proves no one was there when he slipped in."

"Which means he has information that tells him when to strike."

"We're not making any progress." She returned to the chair by the fireplace. "I want to see Doug. I don't want to stay here."

"Okay. We're here. We'll stay the night. It's already Sunday, so you'll have to take Monday off, but we might get you back to work by Tuesday. If Doug agrees."

"Doug has to agree. Maybe Mr. Talbot won't be too angry if I can tell him on Monday that I'll be there on Tuesday. He was adamant that he wanted me there on Monday."

"What's so important about that job?" A legitimate question. "With your qualifications, you could get another one."

"But I'd be looking for a job without any references to help me. I've put seven years of my life into the company. Losing my job would be a total disaster."

"Why?"

"I have to be able to take care of myself."

"Your need for independence." And her ego was involved.

"And I have to go back to my house." She ignored his jab. "Otherwise the killer won't trust whatever is set up."

"Yes. I agree. The security installation should be complete. And I'd continue to spend the nights there. Maybe I can go in and out the back door without him seeing me. Keep him guessing. It's worth a try."

"He may figure out that I'm back and be watching again. I won't sleep much."

"None of us will, until he's caught. But we're going to catch him, before he grabs you."

He picked up the phone and dialed Doug. He answered quickly.

"This guy has to be stopped." He glanced at Tricia. "Time to try something else. Hiding is not working."

"Erik said as much when he called in after dropping you off. But, you're not going to do anything that will endanger Tricia."

Nick sat on the couch. "Of course not. Have the security upgrades been finished at her house?"

"Yes. State of the art. As good as what's out at the house where you are."

"She's ready to go back home and do whatever is necessary to end this ordeal. We're frustrated."

"Okay. I'm calling a meeting of my staff for tomorrow morning. It's a work day. I'm hoping our guy has a job he can't miss and we can operate without detection during office hours."

"What time is the meeting? We both want to be there."

"Tricia needs to stay completely out of sight until a plan is in place. I'll send someone to relieve you so you can come in."

"She'll object."

Tricia stormed across the room. "Let me talk to him." She snatched at the phone. Nick let her have it.

"Uncle Doug, are you trying to keep me away from a meeting? This is my life we're talking about. I want to be there too."

She listened to Doug, then sighed, and handed him the phone.

"Okay, what did you say to her?"

"I don't like it. She's taking too many chances already. But she can come with you if you're both very careful. I'll send Erik for you in the Hummer. You'll use the side entrance to the office. Be careful when you arrive."

"Okay. When can we expect Erik?"

"I'll tell him 8:00. I'll have my staff here by the time you arrive, so we can get started. I'm pulling the entire agency into this. We can't take any chances."

"We'll be ready in the morning."

"Be careful, whatever you do. I'll see you tomorrow. Take care of my girl."

"I'm doing the best I can."

"Make sure you continue to." Doug hung up.

"What else did he say?"

"Erik will be here at eight in the Hummer."

"And we sit here until tomorrow morning." Her frustration showed on her face. "I'm getting tired of trying to keep up with my work when I'm not in the office. I need to figure out who took the bid out of the balance sheet. I need access to people, to email. And a phone I can use."

"But you're alive."

"This isn't living. This is hell." She stomped out of the room.

TO CALM HERSELF DOWN, Tricia took a soothing bath in the Jacuzzi tub. Then she put on another new lounging outfit, a soft jersey knit pantsuit in a mellow teal blue. The texture of the fabric against her skin continued the soothing that had begun in the bath. With her fears and frustrations under a semblance of control, she went downstairs to the living room.

Nick was working, his laptop on the coffee table in front of the leather sectional. A sandwich sat on a plate next to the laptop. A quick hunger pang hit her. A lot had happened since they'd stopped for breakfast in Portland.

She gazed around the big room, at the enormous stone fireplace, the plush leather couch and chairs, the oil paintings on the walls. Did Doug ever spend time out here? She hadn't known this house existed. And Doug had been in Portland for over five years.

By choice she knew very little about her uncle. He was her father's brother. And he hadn't maintained contact with his own two daughters from his first marriage. That had always lowered her opinion of him.

Yet he was doing so much for her. Even bringing Nick up here for her protection. Because she was family. Because she was in trouble. The more she thought about it, the more confused she became.

Nick glanced up when she passed by him on the way to the kitchen. "Good ham in there. Plenty of food. A shame we won't be here to eat it."

"Food isn't important. Getting out of here and back to my house is." She opened the refrigerator door and hauled out the ham and cheese. The refrigerator also contained a rotisserie chicken and deli salads. No need to cook dinner later. Good. She wasn't in the mood.

When her sandwich was ready, she added potato salad to the plate. Then she returned to the living room and sat across from Nick. She ate while he worked. While he concentrated on whatever he was doing. She was getting too used to having him around. That wasn't good.

She liked this older version of the young man from her college days. His maturity fit him. He was intelligent, hardworking, and reliable. He'd shown up at her house on Tuesday evening and today was Sunday. The fifth day. It seemed a lifetime already. Yet they'd be going their separate ways after her stalker was captured. They had no future together.

She finished eating her sandwich and the potato salad, then pushed the plate aside. "Are you finding anything of interest in the dossiers on my former boyfriends?"

"Did you realize Jasper and Pederson used to be smokers?"

"Hmm. No, I didn't. I've always made it clear to the men I've dated that I didn't date smokers. Could they have quit because of me? I don't think so."

"Another reason to interview them again. I was going to personally interview both of them. Having to get you out of the hotel changed those plans. Since the guy had tracked you there. I hope Doug remembers to set up the interviews for tomorrow." He chuckled. "This is the most unorthodox investigation I've ever been involved in. Suits my style."

"Why do you want to talk to them? What have they said?"

"Either one would take you back without hesitation." His brows wrinkled into a puzzling frown. "Do you mesmerize all the guys you're around?"

"Hardly. I don't see you mesmerized." She'd said the words in jest, then regretted them. Heat flared in his eyes.

She jumped up and marched to the window. And stared out at the solid line of fir trees, while willing her heart rate to slow down.

She wanted the comfort of his arms around her. The strength of his body holding her up. Keeping her safe. Yet she knew exactly where that would lead.

Ten long years and it could have been yesterday since they'd last made love.

"Are you okay?" He was standing right behind her.

"No." She could lean into his arms. Instead she leaned forward and touched the glass with her forehead. Cold. She needed warmth, comfort. She needed Nick. But was that fair to him?

He made the choice for her. He grasped her shoulders and turned her around. She walked into his arms. He closed his arms around her, pulling her tight against him. He was fully aroused. He wanted her too.

Her mistake was looking up at him. His mouth slowly descended toward hers. Then his lips were on hers and she opened to him, letting him in, meeting him with equal heat.

His kiss was open-mouthed...wet...hot...and her inner body was steaming in an instant.

She wanted his kiss. And so much more. For a time she could forget the killer, forget Talbot and his threats, forget the fears that stole her peace of mind.

She lost herself in the sensations of having his mouth on hers. The heat radiated through her, settling in her inner core, sparking a need that radiated throughout her body. No man had ever made love to her like Nick.

She pressed against his evident arousal and tangled her fingers in the hair at his nape. Nick growled low in his throat. So why shouldn't they take advantage of this opportunity? They were isolated in the woods, in a house with excellent security. They both wanted the intimacy.

He broke the kiss. "Are you sure? Because if we don't stop now, I won't be able to."

"I don't want you to stop. I want to feel alive." She pulled his head down for another kiss. She couldn't get enough.

By the time they broke apart, both of them were breathing hard. Her own breath came in gasps. What he did to her ought to come with a warning label.

The intensity of his gaze sent goosebumps up her arms. Then he grinned that wicked grin of his that promised so much. His eyes were dark and smoky with desire. He didn't say anything, simply took her hand and drew her toward the stairs. He left his laptop open and on, the remnants of their lunch on the coffee table. She was beyond caring. One thing was on her mind, getting naked with Nick and letting him work his magic. She needed him. For the sex. For the comfort. For the escape.

They reached the top of the stairs and he guided her into his room and over to the bed. He flipped back the spread and covers. She walked into his arms for another long, soul-satisfying kiss.

He was breathing hard, but keeping himself under control. He had always paid attention to her needs, had always been a considerate lover. He grasped the hem of her knit top. And slowly undressed her, taking the time to caress and tease and arouse. She helped him off with his shirt, then he quickly slipped out of his pants and briefs. His shoes had disappeared soon after they'd arrived upstairs.

It had been so long, yet she remembered his body as if it were yesterday. Lean, muscular, enticing.

Once they were both naked, their clothes in heaps on the carpet, Nick reached out one hand and touched her breast, running his finger around the nipple, an erotic gesture so touching tears threatened. He seemed to be worshiping her. Taking his time.

Then he gathered her in his arms for another long kiss. They fell onto the bed while his hands roamed over her sensitive skin.

He broke off the kiss but his eyes sent a scorching message. "We don't have to rush this. This afternoon and the night belong to us."

Was that what she wanted? Was she going to spend the night

in this bed with him? Why not? The comfort of the familiar. Keep the world at bay. She snuggled closer.

He captured her mouth and the kiss deepened, firing her insides and creating ripples of need cascading through her. She couldn't get enough. His lips left her mouth and wandered to her neck and lower. Tantalizing, teasing. Waves of heat swept through her. She arched toward him.

"Slow and easy." He kissed his way across her throat, and lower.

A deeply satisfying sensation spiraled through her. Her breath was labored, and sweat broke out on her body, despite the chill in the room. "I can't stand much more."

He reached into the drawer by the bed and quickly sheathed himself.

He'd come prepared. He'd anticipated this happening. Of course. The ever efficient Nick.

He tugged her close. "How about we start off fast and slow down later?"

She mumbled an agreement.

He positioned himself between her thighs and gently entered her, with easy strokes that drove her wild. She bucked against him. "We'll get there." He thrust again, setting a rhythm she quickly adjusted to. Their bodies had not forgotten.

Higher and higher she soared, the exquisite feelings bombarding her, drawing her out and making her want so much more. A deep, pulsing need sped through her. A need only Nick could satisfy.

"Now," she whispered. And he thrust harder and faster. An explosion of pulsating sensation, then she careened over the edge, in a massive free fall. He followed her down with a gigantic shudder of his own. He collapsed on top of her for a moment, before rolling them to one side.

She clung to him, breathing hard. Suspended in time. Momentarily content. Momentarily satisfied. Unwilling to let the world in.

"I've missed you. I've missed this." He said the words quietly while holding tight to her. "But it can't happen in town, at your house. Too risky."

She nodded. What had been missing from her life was Nick. But he'd go to L.A. She'd stay in Portland. A fleeting stab of regret embedded itself in her heart.

They'd go back to Portland tomorrow. Back where the killer waited. A shudder raced through her.

CHAPTER 17

The rain fell steadily the entire trip to town. Tricia huddled in the backseat of the Hummer, shielded by the darkly tinted windows. Nick rode in the passenger seat up front with Erik. The mood was grim. No conversation for the sake of conversation.

And no heated looks from Nick. The sensual mood of yesterday and last night was long gone.

Erik drove into the lot at the side of the agency building and parked in the empty space nearest the side door. The solid metal-framed door stood closed and forbidding. Tricia shuddered. Nick and Erik got out of the Hummer first, then Nick opened the door for her. She got out. No one was in the parking lot or on the sidewalk.

The agency door opened slowly and Doug limped outside, using his cane, ignoring the rain.

The stone-cold seriousness in Doug's eyes opened a crack in Tricia's resolve. What had she done?

Doug held the door open. Walking through the door meant

commitment to catch the killer. No more hiding. Tricia brushed by Doug and stopped in the hallway.

"I don't like this." His harsh tone widened that crack in her resolve. "I don't want you where this guy can find you. He's too dangerous. Go back to the safe house and stay out of sight until we catch him."

Nick and Erik followed her inside.

She waffled a moment, questioning her motives, but Doug's demeanor couldn't dissuade her. She faced him. "No! I won't hide for the rest of my life because I'm the target of a madman. He won't show himself if I'm gone. I want him caught."

"I've called in my entire staff until this is resolved." He limped through the door and shut it with a decisive thud.

Guilt reared up, but she stomped it down. "Thank you." And she sincerely meant it.

He stared at her for a moment, then limped around the corner to the conference room. She stayed right behind him. Her uncle's help would be the decisive factor. She'd been foolish to think otherwise.

In the conference room the agency investigators and the office receptionist sat around the table. Meagan Fowler, the receptionist, got up and poured her a cup of coffee and handed it to her. "Thanks." Where Doug was, there was always coffee. She knew that much about her uncle.

Tricia took the seat Doug indicated. Nick and Erik got their own coffee and took chairs on the opposite side of the table. With Nick across from her, she could see his eyes, his expression. She'd take her cue from him. She was trusting him with her life. A comforting thought. She did trust him.

Alison Steele's smile radiated pure compassion and she returned the smile automatically. Doug introduced the other four agents as Scott Armstrong, Rafe Campbell, Kara

Rasmussen, and Dave Quinlan. Meagan was off to one side, with her laptop, ready to take notes.

Doug refilled his coffee cup, then sat at his place at one end of the table. "Thanks to the DNA matches, our suspect has been identified as a serial killer. What we don't have is a name." His gaze lit on each person surrounding the table. "We have complete FBI assistance. Special Agent Edward Thompson, from the local office, is leading the task force assembled to catch this guy. We're not officially a part of the task force, but they're welcoming our help. Chet Richardson, the lead detective assigned to this case, will have access to all the resources of the Portland Police Bureau."

Tricia squirmed in her chair. What had she set in motion? No, not her. The killer started this, long before he came to Portland. She was going to be part of the finish.

But the Uncle Doug she'd known for years had disappeared. The man in his place was all business, wearing his serious expression like a badge. He had the respect of his entire staff. He had a reputation for getting the job done.

"Tricia, I realize this has been difficult for you," Doug said, "but I want you to fully understand what you and Nick are wanting. And the consequences."

"I know the consequences." She lifted her chin. "If this guy isn't caught, someone is going to die. Maybe me, maybe another woman, if he gets tired of waiting for me to come out of hiding."

"I want this guy caught, before he harms anyone else." Nick's tone was laced with anger.

"I do, too." Doug took a sip of his coffee. "So we have to come up with a foolproof plan to protect Tricia and get our man. First we have to figure out who he is."

"We have to flush him out." Tricia set down her coffee cup. "I have to go back to a normal routine, back to my house, back to work, where he can see me."

"That's the dangerous part." Doug stood and pushed his chair back. "I don't see any other way. But, I don't like it." He limped to the white board at one end of the room. "I don't want you in danger. I don't want you hurt."

Tricia's heart swelled. Her uncle cared deeply. Before the stalker, she thought he didn't. She'd always assumed he was like her father because they were brothers. When this was over, she hoped to get to know him better.

"Okay, first thing, someone will be in the office with Tricia. Not Nick. The guy has seen him too much." Doug wrote Tricia's name on one end of the white board. "Alison was out of town until Saturday. She gets the assignment as Tricia's daily bodyguard, but we're infiltrating her into the office as seamlessly as possible." He wrote her name next to Tricia's.

"Could he have seen Alison on Saturday, when he planted the GPS on the Beemer?" Nick asked.

"It's possible. But if he's been outside this office for any length of time, he's seen my entire staff. I can't bring in anyone else on such short notice." He hesitated a moment. Then glanced at Alison. "Besides, she's the best shot in the agency."

Interesting. A look, not of envy, but of pride.

"Alison will start work there today, and be in place whenever Tricia is there. I've made the arrangements with her boss and he's cleared it with human resources. Nick will take Tricia to the office in the morning, and pick her up and drive her home. Then he'll leave, and enter the house from the rear. He'll take over and stay the night."

The first glimmer of hope rose inside Tricia. But was quickly crushed by doubt. Why would Talbot agree? Was he sincere in wanting the problem solved? She shook her head to clear those thoughts.

She was no longer alone, feeling violated and vulnerable. On her side were Doug and his team, including Nick. Plus the police. Plus the FBI. The fear deep inside gnawed at her, but that embryonic hope was there too.

Doug wrote the other names of his agents on the board, with their assignments. "Catching this guy before he can grab Tricia is number one priority. We have to get him to do something that reveals who he is. Nothing else matters. Understood?"

A murmur of agreement blanketed the room.

"Erik, stay at the computer and tackle the tech end of the investigation. We can't spare you for any more field work unless it involves your expertise."

"How do I get in and out of Tricia's house? What's behind the house?" Nick asked.

Doug pointed to Scott Armstrong.

Scott nodded. "I'll be there. A gate opens onto a short alley. You'll park in the next block. In a lot. Come down the alley. Enter through the gate."

Doug handed Nick a set of keys. "Your new SUV is parked up the street in the next block." He pointed toward the side street that ran by the agency. "Dark charcoal gray." Doug laughed, but it was a forced laugh. "I didn't want it parked in our lot."

"Good thinking. Thanks."

Tricia's respect for Doug's plan grew. Scott was dressed like a gardener or someone who'd be working outside. He had a slightly scruffy appearance. Longish wavy brown hair, a two-day beard growth. Dave Quinlan resembled a biker. Leathers. Had she seen a motorcycle outside when they'd come in? The only one who appeared professional was Rafe Campbell. He was dressed in slacks and sport coat. Nick had told her he was the one assigned to question anyone Chet Richardson didn't have time for.

"Tricia," Doug said. "Before we go any further, are you sure you want to do this. You can back out at any time and go on an extended vacation."

She hesitated before answering, to make sure her voice was steady and didn't betray any of her hidden fears. "I was never more sure. I like what you've outlined. I feel better and more confident that we can catch him."

He gazed at her, but didn't say anything more to her. "Nick, will this plan work for you?" A business-like tone.

"Yes." Warmth glowed in the depth of Nick's eyes. "We'll protect her. When we spot anything wrong, we can quickly step in."

"Okay. Tricia moves back to her house today. She can go shopping again, if she wants to. With Nick. Then Nick takes her home and leaves the house by the front door and reenters through the back. Scott will get their luggage from the Hummer and take it to the house, going through the back door."

"What kind of security system was installed?" She drained her coffee cup.

"State of the art." Scott passed her a slip of paper with the code written on it. And instructions for use. "Your house is a technological fortress with a direct link to the security company. Any breach of security and the police will be notified immediately. Including the nearest patrol car."

"That sounds good."

"And the locks were changed again. You and Nick will have keys to the house, along with Doug."

"Memorize the code, then destroy the paper." Doug sat at the table. "Before you leave here."

Nick appeared pensive and Tricia wondered what he was thinking. Was he worrying or was he pleased this plan was going forward?

"Alison is ready to go to work, once you give her more information," Doug said.

"I'll start the day at the secretary support desk outside your office," Alison said. "But when you arrive, I'll be inside your office with you and go anywhere you go."

"And if anything happens, she'll be right beside you, ready to defend you." Doug picked up his coffee cup and took a sip.

Tricia couldn't help feeling overwhelmed. This was getting complicated.

"If we're lucky, the guy will show his hand immediately and we'll nail him," Doug said. "Nick, you'll interview Jasper and Pederson tomorrow, while Tricia is working. Okay team, you have your assignments." Everyone rose.

Tricia passed near Doug and he stopped her. Drew her into his arms. She couldn't remember ever being hugged by her uncle. Tears formed behind her eyes and she willed them away. She couldn't show any sign of weakness around him, or he'd call off the plan.

"You take care." He let her go. "You and Alison go sit over there." He indicated the chairs in the corner. "You can bring her up to speed on your daily routine. Then she's out of here."

Tricia moved to the corner chair as Nick left the conference room. Her chest constricted in a moment of panic. A silly reaction. She was safe at the agency. Alison sat next to her. "Okay, let's get started." She kept her tone decisive.

NICK SLIPPED into Doug's office and shut the door. Doug was leaning against the window sill, his expression grim.

"Sending Tricia back to work in that office building could be a huge mistake." Doug pushed away from the window and picked up a small stack of pages from his desk. "I don't trust the security there."

"I don't either."

"You'd better not screw up."

"Is that why Alison is her bodyguard during the day?" His ever-present guilt rose to the surface.

"Part of it. But you're going to be doing detective work. Something that you're good at."

Nick's gut twisted like he'd been punched. He'd let Doug down.

Doug handed Nick the pages. "This is what I didn't want Tricia to see."

Nick took the pages and skimmed through them quickly, stunned by the graphic detail in the report. "A torture chamber in a white panel truck." He said the words with disgust. "Do you realize how many white panel trucks there are in the city of Portland?"

"I have a vague idea." Doug sat behind his desk and steepled his fingers.

Nick waited for him to process his thoughts.

Tricia was family, which made it doubly difficult for him. Doug was a compassionate person who didn't like violence. He'd become a cop for the right reasons. To fight violence. Protect other people. Get justice for victims. The same reason Nick had become a cop. And his father before him.

"The FBI found a vacant house in Chicago where the guy had been hiding out." Anger rode Doug's words. "And a journal where he'd methodically recorded how long it took each of the first five women to die after he started slicing on them. He kept an assortment of lethal knives in the truck. Once they were dead, he rolled them in a carpet remnant and buried them in the woods. They weren't found until animals dug them up, sometimes months later."

"He must have left Chicago suddenly. Why did he leave the journal behind?"

"He did leave in a hurry. The remote spot where he took his sixth victim wasn't remote enough. A hiker heard her screams. The guy was wearing a ski mask when he ran the hiker off with a couple of shots. Then he slit the woman's throat, dumped her out of the truck, and drove off. And presumably kept on driving."

"Maybe straight to Portland. So if we spot a white panel truck anywhere near her house, we check it out."

"Right. And Dave is going on patrol to see how many he can find. He's looking for an Illinois license plate or stolen plates."

"You don't think Tricia ought to be warned about the white panel truck?"

"No. She's not going to be alone until the guy is caught. She'd ask more questions if she knew."

"I still think she has a right to know."

"No, she doesn't. These are details kept out of the media in the cities where the murders took place. Investigators keep back information known only to them and the culprit."

"That makes sense. If it doesn't end up somehow hurting us and our plan."

Doug stood. "It's for her own good. Take her shopping, then home. Call Chet immediately if anything happens." He reached out his hand. "Good luck."

They shook hands. "I'll take care of her, Doug."

"See that you do. Be doubly careful, doubly aware, doubly vigilant."

Doug's tone stung. The full weight of his obligation to Doug and to Tricia hit him with full force. Her life depended on him. On all of them.

CHAPTER 18

*N*ick braked to a stop in front of Tricia's house. She got out of the SUV and grabbed her shopping bags. "Reset the alarm after you're inside. I'll reset it again when I come in the back, after I park the car. Stay alert."

Her withering look said she didn't need the reminder.

Once she was inside the house, he drove around the block twice, checking for anyone who didn't belong in the area. Or any white panel trucks. He parked the SUV in a gravel lot behind a row of hedges. His designated parking spot arranged by Doug. With briefcase in hand, he walked down the alley, dodged a green dumpster, and entered the yard through the gate. Scott was raking leaves near the fence. He didn't speak or acknowledge him in any way.

Nick used the two keys to get into the laundry room and the kitchen, then punched in the alarm code on the pad. Then he walked into the living room and set down his briefcase. Tricia stood near her dining room table, her mail scattered across the oak surface. She appeared startled when she heard him.

"What's wrong?"

"Another letter. There." She pointed to a brown envelope on top. "And messages on the answering machine."

Tension radiated from her body. He resisted taking her into his arms. They had to stay alert. He'd keep his distance as best he could.

"Let's deal with the mail first." He went to the kitchen for a plastic bag, then used a smaller plastic sandwich bag to pick up the letter, so his fingerprints wouldn't be on it, though he doubted the killer had been careless enough to leave his own.

Tricia backed away from the table and the envelope. He took out his pocket knife, slit the envelope, and carefully removed the piece of paper and a picture of the two of them at the falls. His gut twisted into a tight knot. The killer had used a powerful zoom lens. There was no mistaking who was in the picture.

He laid the paper and photo on the table. On the page, in big block letters made with a marking pen, the words stood out. "I found you. I'll find you again. Then you die."

He heard her intake of breath and saw her shudder. She ducked her head, her face pale. Then she picked up her shopping bags and headed upstairs without a word. Her pace quickened as she got closer to the top of the stairs. She needed time alone and he didn't blame her. It rattled him to see the letter too. The guy was still out there, still not letting them forget him.

Still causing trouble for both of them. When Doug saw the picture of them kissing, he'd realize Nick hadn't kept his promise to keep to business. He couldn't hide the picture and pretend it didn't exist. He'd be guilty of concealing evidence.

He made a quick call to Chet and told him about the letter and picture. Chet said he'd be by in a couple of hours to pick them up.

Tricia came downstairs a few minutes later, no longer pale and shaking. She'd regained her composure. He admired her courage.

"Okay, I'm ready to listen to the messages." She stayed where she was, across the room from the machine.

There were four messages, according to the readout. He punched the button and listened to all four, one from a Jane Mobley, who wanted to meet Tricia for lunch, one from her hairdresser to reschedule the appointment she'd missed, and two of those nuisance scam calls. None from the killer. He knew they hadn't been there if he'd been watching the house.

"I'll have to call Jane and tell her it's not a good time."

"Wait a day or two. She called last Friday and hasn't heard from you yet, so would assume you're not available."

"I hope she doesn't think I'm ignoring her. She was a good friend when she worked at Talbot."

"Remember, no deviations from the plan. We take no chances."

"Jane's a friend." Tricia's voice pleaded.

"No deviations."

"You're right." She heaved a big sigh. "You're in detective mode, and working a case. I'm part of it, because I'm the victim and the bait. I'll stick to the script."

"It's almost lunchtime." He changed the subject on purpose. "Let's see if anyone thought to get the food from the safe house and bring it here." He went to the kitchen and opened the refrigerator. And was rewarded with the sight of a spiral ham and three containers of deli salads. As well as eggs, bacon, sodas, orange juice, etc. Bread on the counter. "A new supply. Someone's still shopping for us."

Tricia brushed by him. "At least we won't starve, thanks to Doug's efficiency."

He touched her arm, wanting the contact.

She walked into his embrace. Then stiffened. "Not a good idea." She slipped out of his arms.

"Sorry. I promise I'll stick to business."

He headed for the living room. "Back to work. I have files to access and data to input and analyze. Also things I couldn't do out there without internet access."

She followed him. "I'll start by putting away the new things I bought, then I'll come down and fix us each a plate." She glanced up the stairs. "How has my life spun completely out of control in such a short time?"

He understood what she was saying. They were alike in wanting control, wanting their lives to unfold in a predictable manner.

What had been set in motion in Doug's conference room was anything but a sure thing. The wild card was the guy who'd started it all, whoever he was. The killer was in control.

ALONE IN HER ROOM, Tricia sank down on her bed, on the stiff new mattress that had been delivered over the weekend. She buried her face in her hands and breathed deeply, to ease her rising panic.

Another letter. And that picture. He wasn't giving up, merely increasing the pressure until it was almost unbearable. When would this nightmare end?

She no longer enjoyed her usual sense of safety and pleasure in her home. Her stalker had taken her feelings of security along with the belongings he'd destroyed.

When she'd moved in, she'd decorated the bedroom for her comfort, in shades of soft blue, chosen because they made her feel peaceful. That peaceful feeling was gone. The bedspread she'd spent hours shopping for had been replaced with something she'd chosen quickly, merely a substitute for the one he'd mutilated.

Her personal tastes were no longer important. Her priority was getting back to work to save her job. And help catch the killer.

She heard the ring tone of Nick's cell phone, from downstairs. She didn't understand what he was saying, though she could tell by the sound of his voice he was upset. She resisted the urge to hurry down to see if something else had happened.

She needed to put away the new clothes and accessories she'd bought earlier. The stacks sat on the bed from where she'd taken them out of their bags. She jumped up from the bed and picked up the underwear. And the bathrobe she'd finally remembered to buy.

She hoped she hadn't made a mistake coming back home. Hiding and hoping the killer would give up was tempting. When they were out of town, they'd had a respite from the tension. A small sigh escaped. Making love to Nick was a mistake, though it had felt right at the time. She'd remember yesterday afternoon and evening for years. Because there would not be a repeat.

The guy had broken into her house twice and started a fire in a hotel. What else could he do? She shuddered. She didn't want to know, didn't want to think about it, didn't want to think about who he was and how soon he could be caught. Thinking led to more frustration.

And what about Nick? Would he leave immediately for Los Angeles as soon as the guy was arrested? Or would he stick around, and support her through a trial? Would he want more than she was willing to give? She had questions, but not a single answer.

She closed the closet door and the open drawers. That job was done. Then she quickly made up the bed with the new sheets and blanket she'd bought today, and the bedspread she bought on Friday.

When she descended the stairs, Nick was still on the phone, though he no longer sounded upset.

"I've got to go. I'll talk to you later." He ended the call and focused on his computer, ignoring her.

"Who have you been talking to?" She reached the bottom of the stairs and crossed to the couch.

"Nothing about the case."

"Then why are you looking so guilty?" She said the words in jest.

"It was a private conversation. Something I had to take care of." His words were abrupt, delivered in a don't-bother-me tone.

"You aren't going to tell me." A quiet statement, not a question.

"No, I'm not." He pushed his computer to the side and headed for the kitchen, dismissing the subject. And her.

Her heart constricted, reminding her of the situation she'd gotten herself into. Committed partners didn't keep secrets. She and Nick were casual lovers who happened to be stuck with each other for a while. It bothered her more than it should.

NICK'S STOMACH CHURNED. He held the refrigerator door open, staring at the food inside, yet not seeing it. He'd upset Tricia by not telling her about the phone call. But he was too upset to talk about it rationally.

Yet, keeping secrets from her might not be such a bad idea. If she stayed upset with him, it built the barrier between them a bit higher. He should never have made love to her. That barrier should have stayed in place until she was safe and he could leave Portland. A future with her was not going to happen.

"Are you getting out the food for lunch?" She stood in the doorway, like she was afraid to come in. Her vulnerabilities were highlighted in the depth of her expressive brown eyes.

"Yes." He grabbed the ham and potato salad, then the mayonnaise and mustard. She opened the sour dough bread on the counter and got out plates and silverware.

They worked silently, side by side, fixing their lunches. He tried to ignore her subtle fragrance, the pure essence of her that had haunted him for years. Being around her every day reminded him of what he particularly liked about her. That subtle fragrance, her flowing brown hair, the expressiveness of those dark eyes, her pure sensuality. And he wanted her again.

A thought kicked him in the head. He wanted that future with her that he couldn't have.

He followed her back to the living room and sat on the opposite end of the couch from her. He ignored her and opened his laptop. He used his right hand to tap the keys to where he wanted to go in the database while he held his sandwich with the other hand. With sheer willpower he focused on what he was seeing and put her out of his mind. When thoughts of her crept in, he booted them out.

He worked that way for over an hour, completely engrossed in the search for information on the killings attributed to the suspect. He stretched and rolled his shoulders to loosen them up. Tricia was standing in the doorway to the dining room.

"My boss hasn't called today. I wish I knew what was going on." Her voice sounded strained. Not the forceful tone she usually used.

"You'll be going to work tomorrow and have access to the people with the answers for you." He stood and paced back and forth. Time for a break from the computer.

Her half laugh contained no mirth. "If anyone will give me the information I need."

"You must have someone on your side, after working there so long." He stopped next to the table.

"I guess I'll find out tomorrow." She glanced around. "Where's the rest of my mail?"

"On the little desk. Chet is coming for the letter and picture that are in that plastic bag on the table."

She visibly shuddered and moved farther from the plastic bag.

"Everything is getting so complicated." Her voice held a plaintive tone.

"Investigative work is always complicated. We have to sift through the facts and stay alert for new developments. The culprit acts. We react. We have to wrest control from him and capture him."

"I hope you do. Soon." She sorted through her mail, then put it in a desk drawer. "What happens next?"

"We wait and watch and hope he does something to give us a clue who he is. Then we take him down."

"Sounds simple. I go to work, act as bait, wonder which of the many men I see daily wants to kill me."

Her expression was cloaked in bleakness. He wished he had words to bolster her confidence. He wished he could provide the physical comfort she needed. To protect his own sanity, all he could do was remain vigilant.

CHAPTER 19

*T*ricia rode the elevator to the eighth floor the next morning, Nick at her side. When the elevator stopped, he held the button to keep the door closed. "I don't like leaving you here. Even if Alison is with you." His concern for her was written boldly on his features. The pursed lips. The scowl. The hard eyes.

The butterflies in her stomach did their own little dance. "We both have jobs to do today. Don't worry." She pasted on a false smile.

"Be careful. If anything feels wrong, don't hesitate to tell Alison. Call one of us on the phone if someone or something should be checked out."

"I'll be okay." She gazed at him and hoped she was right. He let the door open and she stepped out. The door closed on Nick and panic seized her, squeezing her lungs, cutting off her air. She took a deep breath, then another, taking her time. The panic slowly eased.

She crossed the upper lobby into the offices of Talbot Enterprises, her legs like lead. Her lack of energy could be because of little sleep lately, but dread also accompanied her, and that occasional wave of panic.

She walked through the office area and exchanged greetings with the people she passed. No one said anything about why she'd been gone for two days or mentioned her desk that had been slashed and defaced. They must have been told it was random vandalism. The fewer who knew she was being stalked by a killer, the better. So she could do her job.

Alison sat at a desk outside Tricia's office door, her shoulder length blond hair curving around her face. She looked like a professional office worker. They exchanged casual hellos, then Alison picked up her coffee cup and the papers she was sorting and joined Tricia in her office.

"You're tense. Try to relax." Alison pushed a chair up to the table next to the desk. "We'll get through this. Trust Doug. Trust Nick."

Tricia heaved a big sigh. "I want it to be over. We had to come back here to make that happen."

"I think you're right. Just for the record." She smiled.

Alison was alert, she was armed, and a crack shot. The loose jacket she wore covered the holster on her belt. Nick had filled her in on the woman's qualifications last night.

Tricia locked up her purse and set her briefcase on her desk, far from the scar left by the deep gouge. She shivered, then forced herself to sit in her chair. Strange sensations overtook her. Agitation. A slight panicky feeling. She ran her hand over the refinished wood surface. An image of the broad slash of red surfaced. She shuddered, then recoiled.

Her computer was completely off, not in locked sleep mode. Her chest constricted. Someone had been in here. Was it someone from the finance department, snooping for any information she had? But they wouldn't have her password.

She tapped the button to turn on her computer, still puzzling over why it had been turned off. The reboot finished and she put in her password. And the desktop came into view. She jumped up and stifled a scream. Her heart rate soared into overdrive, pounding in her chest. A bold message had been superimposed on the desktop: "You can't hide. You're mine."

Alison responded immediately, shutting the door and getting between her and the door. "What is it?"

For a moment Tricia was numb with fright, unable to speak. She pointed at the computer screen.

"Your nemesis came back."

"Whoever it is has complete access to my office. And my computer. He got past my password." She squeaked out the words. "First the desk, now the computer."

"Could the message have been missed on Friday?"

"It's possible. I didn't have time to do anything on the computer before I had to leave."

Alison took out her cell phone. "I'm calling Doug. Erik can figure out when this was done."

"Good. I don't trust the tech people in this building. Whoever the guy is, he can get in here when he wants."

When Alison finished explaining to Doug, she handed her phone to Tricia.

"Hi, Uncle Doug."

"Erik is on his way. Don't say anything to anyone. The fewer people who are aware what's going on, the better." He echoed her own thoughts. "I'll alert Nick and have him take you to lunch when he's finished the interviews, so you can compare notes."

"Thanks. I'm feeling jumpy this morning and I haven't even started working."

"Hang in there. We'll find this guy."

"Thanks, Uncle Doug. It's such a relief to have you there, and Nick, and Alison. The rest of your staff. I feel safer even though I may not be."

"Don't let your guard down. We don't have him yet."

Her chest constricted. "You're right. I'll stay alert."

"Don't touch any keys until Erik gets there."

"I won't." She ended the call. Then sat to the side of the desk. She had paper files she could access while she waited for Erik. Plenty to do. Her heart pounded faster than normal, and the tension headache that had been hovering for days had begun its relentless throbbing.

Thirty minutes later she stood behind her desk chair, while Erik worked his magic.

"This guy's good," Erik said. He punched a few more keys, and repeated his diagnostic routine. "He got past your password and added the desktop file without leaving anything to lead us to him. It wasn't a hacker from outside the system. This was done from your computer."

His hazel eyes were sympathetic. He was the youngest man on the team and had a fresh, youthful appearance that contradicted his age and wisdom.

"I didn't want it to be someone here in the office." She leaned closer. "Can you tell when the message was added? Whether it was last Friday?"

"Access was on Friday, but at night. Not in the morning."

"Oh. After the desk was fixed."

"I'm almost positive." Erik stood. "I'll report this to Doug. We need to check the backgrounds of everyone in this tall building. A tall order."

She laughed at his attempt at humor. Though it wasn't funny. There were far too many people in an office building of this size, comprising many businesses. "Nick's coming for me at noon and we're having lunch at the grill on tenth. He'll fill me in on what's happening, I guess."

"Why don't Rafe and I join you? We're both working this morning. I'll be on the computer and Rafe on the interviews."

"Good idea." And the two of them would be a buffer between her and Nick. Though she doubted there was anything left of their tenuous relationship.

As soon as Erik left, Tricia sat down at her computer, afraid to touch the keys. But she had work to do. She took a deep, calming breath and reached for her laptop instead.

She'd written a memo to Mr. Talbot the night before, that explained in detail the missing bid and how the spreadsheet was manipulated to cover up the loss of funds. She sent the memo off by email, hoping her explanation would satisfy him and get him to search for the culprit himself. Unless he was involved in the cover up.

She wouldn't give up yet, but would fight for her job. If he did nothing, that would be confirmation he didn't want the truth. That his objective was to fire her.

NICK AND TRICIA joined Erik and Rafe at a table in the far corner of the restaurant, and ordered their lunches.

Nick took a sip of water, then set down the glass. "Let's summarize. Our suspect works in the building. We don't know where or what he does. He's been there less than six months. The last murder was in April, in Chicago."

"At least that we're aware of." Rafe's tone reeked of skepticism. Rafe was older than anyone else in the agency, other than Doug. Well-groomed and suave when he wanted to be, he fit in anywhere. Yet he was an ex-cop from New York and street tested. A good man to have on the team.

Tricia was fiddling with her napkin and squirming in her chair. Nick glanced at her, then back at Rafe. "You're right. But until we find out differently, we'll assume he came here after that murder. And has access to Tricia's office."

Their drinks were served and Erik took a sip of his soda. Then set it down. "The slashed desk was found Friday morning. The message Tricia found today was put on the computer Friday evening, after the desk was repaired."

Nick mulled over the information. "You're sure about the timing on the message?"

Erik nodded.

The server arrived with their salads.

"It couldn't have been done earlier than eight o'clock," Tricia said. "I checked the backups this morning. The routine is automatic, controlled by the system. He waited until after it had run, then added the message. He's familiar with the system." Her voice was shaky.

Nick didn't blame her. She'd been through a rough few days and holding up better than he had expected. Testament to her inner strength.

Rafe set down his fork. "We're dealing with someone who's computer savvy, intelligent, and has seemingly unlimited access."

"That's the conclusion I came to." Nick let his anger show in his tone.

Rafe nodded. "Chet and the FBI agent, Thompson, are getting the employee records for the entire building, even if it takes a court order to get all businesses to comply with the request. We ought to have them within a couple of days."

Tricia set down her glass of soda. "Rafe, are you interviewing the Talbot employees? Doug had the list already."

"Yes. I began with the latest hires. I'm getting complete cooperation from the elder Talbot, Jerome. Even though he's been out of the country, he's been in touch with the police. He wants this cleared up fast."

"I've started my online searches on the Talbot employees too," Erik said. "So far nothing stands out, even in the private databases, but I'll keep looking."

"Rafe, are you interviewing the people hired in May and June? Since we know the latest murder was in April." Nick forked a bite of salad.

"That's what I've been working on this morning."

"We need to check on anyone who could possibly have a reason to be on the eighth floor at any time. Including support staff, such as janitorial."

"I'll resume the computer searches on the Talbot employee list as soon as I get back to the agency," Erik said. "I'll take the ones that have already been run and compile the information and have reports ready before I leave for the night. And each day I'll do a report of what I've accomplished that day."

"Good," Nick said. "We can't let anyone slip past our scrutiny. We'll check and double check everyone."

"The building has twelve stories. That's a lot of businesses and a lot of people employed there." Tricia's expression was grim. "He could strike at any time and it could take weeks to process the long lists of people through this system."

"We have one crucial bit of information we didn't have before." Nick set down his glass. "Approximate time of hire is our most important piece of data. Eliminates a lot of people."

"That fact narrows our search criteria." Erik shoved his empty salad bowl to the side. "I redesigned the search algorithms yesterday."

The server arrived with their lunches and the conversation stopped. Tricia nibbled at her fish fillet, taking a few bites, then putting down her fork. She was visibly disturbed by this latest intrusion on her privacy. Not even her office computer protected by a password was out of the reach of this madman.

As Nick had learned during years of police work, stalkers enjoyed terrorizing their victims. This guy had Tricia spooked. Tension lined her face. She sat stiffly in the chair, not relaxing to enjoy her lunch. And he could do nothing to comfort her. He picked up his sandwich and took a bite.

Erik jotted a few notes on a pad. "Okay, I'll keep working on the Talbot employees and try to finish them by the time I get the other lists from Chet and Ed Thompson. If we start with those who work on the eighth floor, then the support staff for the building itself, that will further narrow the search."

"If our guy isn't simply a rogue. Operating by his own set of rules." Another skeptical comment from Rafe. "How many people have access to passkeys of any kind for the building? Another list to make."

"The lists will be long." Nick grimaced. "But it's the best we can do. We'll include maintenance people, janitorial staff, security personnel, building administrators and their staff."

"Anyone with access," Erik said.

"Tricia, did you pick up on anything today?" Nick put down his fork. She was staring at the table, not eating.

"Nothing." She looked up. "Not a clue. No one is acting suspicious. No sign of stress in anyone that I can see."

"Stay vigilant. We'll check out anything signaling a problem."

He pierced her with a stare. "Even something small and seemingly insignificant could be the key to finding this guy."

"What are Kara and Dave Quinlan doing?" Tricia asked. "What are their roles?"

The three men exchanged glances. Tricia's eyes blazed with sudden anger. He braced for her outburst. Not telling her about the white panel truck could get tricky.

She scowled. "What are you guys keeping from me? You're wearing guilty expressions."

Nick exhaled but didn't answer the accusation. "Kara will help as a bodyguard when she's needed. She's also night relief for me tonight so I can get some sleep. She'll be at the house about ten. Dave is doing surveillance out on his bike, looking for suspicious activity." They wouldn't tell her he was checking for a white panel truck near the office building or her house.

"We're searching for any clue, no matter how insignificant," Rafe said. "We have a good team, we have intelligence, all we need is a bit of luck." He shrugged. "Our break might come today."

Tricia's scowl remained firmly in place.

Nick picked up the last of his sandwich. "We can't give up hope. We'll catch him." He took a bite, but watched the expression on Tricia's face.

She suspected they were hiding information from her. He only hoped she didn't find out how sadistic the suspect was. The stuff of nightmares.

CHAPTER 20

*T*he street light out front cast eerie shadows in the darkened living room. Tricia stood by the couch and listened. She was finally home, yet not feeling secure.

Nick was parking the SUV. He'd be here in a few minutes.

She set down her briefcase and purse. Then drew the drapes, shutting out the shadows, before flipping on the lights. Nothing had been disturbed while she was gone. The guy hadn't been back. Not that he could get past the security system without alerting the police.

Ten minutes later Nick arrived. She met him in the kitchen.

"Are you okay?" His expression was pure compassion.

"Yes. No. I'm no longer comfortable in my own house."

He reached for her and pulled her against his chest. "I've wanted to do this all day. Let me hold you for a minute."

She stiffened. Why was she back in his arms?

"Relax. I'm simply reassuring myself you're all right. I promise you. No expectations."

She settled against him, let the heat from his body penetrate the chill surrounding her. The pressure of his solid muscles radiated the strength she desperately needed. His arms made her feel safe, at least for the moment.

He released her. "Guess it wasn't such a good idea."

She backed away from him. "No it wasn't." Then she trailed after him, into the living room, snapping on more lights.

"I need to print out several pages." His tone had changed to brusque. "Erik sent me his report on the Talbot employees and I'd like a hard copy so I can mark it up. I assume you have a printer somewhere?" He took out his laptop and pushed his briefcase aside.

The abrupt change of subject left her feeling disjointed. Okay, back to business. She could do it too. "Bring your laptop."

She headed down the hallway, to a door near the rear of the house. "My printer is in the office I rarely use." She opened the door and crossed to the oak desk. "You can set your laptop here." She pushed folders and a book out of the way.

He booted his laptop, retrieved the file, and the printer connected through the wifi. The pages accumulated quickly in the hopper. Would the answers be there? Not likely. She didn't expect the culprit to be a Talbot employee, since she didn't feel like she was being watched when she was inside the offices. When she was outside, on the street and in other places, the eerie feeling that someone was there, watching her, had spooked her more than once.

"Oh, I finally interviewed Jasper and Pederson this after-noon," Nick said. "Caught up with them where they couldn't avoid me." His lips quirked into a self-satisfied smirk. "But they're clean as we expected. Neither wanted their relationship with you to end. Their only gripe."

"If you expected it, why question them?"

"We'd already eliminated anyone who'd been in Portland

over six months. Interviewing them closed that part of the investigation. A good investigator checks everything."

"It's a relief that Rob and Andy are cleared. I didn't want it to be someone I've cared for, even if I did break off the relationship."

"What were you running from?" He said the words quietly, but with an emotional undertone.

The question jolted her. She'd denied running when he asked earlier. Could she get by with an evasive answer? She decided on honesty. "Myself. My own fears. I don't do permanent. I told you that."

"Yes, I remember. And I remember how much it hurt. I know how Andy and Rob are feeling." A stab of censure flowed through her. Okay, she was lousy at relationships. Should she avoid men altogether?

"But you haven't kept your distance." Her tone accused. "You started with kisses. And you didn't stop. We can't undo what we've done."

"I'm already regretting it. I want much more than you're willing to give. I always have." He picked up the stack of pages from the hopper. Then his laptop. "Let's go."

A pang of guilt knifed through her. She'd end up hurting him again. Back in the living room, she sank down in the chair across from the couch. Nick focused on the pages he'd printed. She'd be hurting too when the suspect was caught and Nick returned to his job in L.A. She'd never forget the feeling of closeness and satisfaction making love with him again had given her. Only Nick gave her that kind of contentment. Yet he was guarding his heart this time. Okay, she'd continue to keep her distance and make it easier on him. And harder on her.

He raised his eyes to meet her gaze. "Out at the falls, you

said you avoided permanent because of the way your father treated your mother."

"That's part of it. But not all. It's me. I've never trusted a man to be there for me."

"Because your dad wasn't there for your mother."

"He was never there for me either, when I was growing up." She heaved a sigh. "And when he left, my mother withdrew emotionally. I was alone."

"You're so afraid of getting hurt that you do the hurting first. Then you can justify leaving because you're protecting yourself."

The truth stung. She'd seen her mother need her father and vowed she'd never need a man. Childhood lessons that clung long beyond childhood. She couldn't simply change. She was destined to be alone, except for fleeting relationships.

Up until Nick came back into her life, she hadn't found anyone worth staying with. Ten years ago she didn't realize what a catch he was. She'd ruined her chances with him then. Too late now, yet she was falling further and further in love with him. How could she have let it happen?

"You're right. I am afraid." She stood. "I'm going upstairs for a while." She rationalized that he'd get more work done without her to distract him. Yet she needed to distance herself from him and the hold he had over her. The mess she was in was her own fault. How do you stop loving a man before he changes the life you've carefully built?

THE PHONE RANG. Nick hesitated, waiting to see if Tricia picked it up in the bedroom. She let it ring.

He checked caller ID. Blocked. He picked up the phone and pushed the record button. "Yes."

"Get out of her house. You're making me angry." The low growly voice made the threats more eerie. Nick listened, trying to get a fix on the man through his use of words. Nothing out of the ordinary in his speech patterns. When the guy hung up, Nick immediately called the police and had them check the trace on the line.

Ten minutes later Chet called. "A disposable cell phone."

"Damn. Of course he'd use a prepaid. Thanks, Chet." He hung up.

Tricia had come downstairs and into the room. "It was him, wasn't it?"

"Yes. I'm sorry. He hasn't given up. Since I answered, he knows I'm here."

"Let me hear it."

He turned on the recorder. She moved closer to listen. She visibly drew into herself, hugging her body with her arms. Even a strong woman like Tricia was affected by such threats.

"I'll call Doug. He'll want to know." He took out his cell phone and punched in the number. Tricia sat down on the couch, staring across the room, eyes unfocused.

Nick told Doug about the call.

"Any way to trace it?"

"Chet said it's a disposable cell phone. But, the guy's definitely angry. Maybe he'll start making mistakes."

"Play the recording for me, and put the phone next to it. I want to hear this one."

Nick did as he asked.

"Okay, I think you're right. He's angry, lashing out, and admits it. We have to watch for someone to slip up and point a finger at himself."

Nick's gut clenched. "If we have enough people around to see any mistake he makes. If we can catch him." Too many ifs.

"He won't make a mistake." Resignation rode Tricia's voice. "He's been too careful."

"Remember," Doug said, "we also have the DNA match with the six other killings, which gives us another way to check. We're making progress. Don't give up hope."

"That's right." Nick ended the call.

"What's right?" Tricia stood directly in front of him.

"We have two criteria to check, because of the DNA match with the other killings."

She was quiet a minute, obviously thinking. "Okay, but how much time is this going to take? We have a long list of people who have access to my office."

"True. Erik has the database to analyze the information collected. His analysis should go faster now. We ought to find a match soon."

"I hope you're right." She picked up the report he'd been reading, the one from Erik. "Anything here we can use?"

"Not yet. Not until we have some matches."

The phone rang again.

She visibly shuddered. "You answer it."

Nick picked up the phone. "The security firm." He answered and dropped down on the end of the couch.

"Someone in a hooded ski mask showed up on the surveillance video from earlier today. About 2:00 am. Thought you'd want that information."

"We certainly do. Can you tell us anything else? What else he was wearing? Can you estimate how tall he is?"

"He was dressed in black. Including ski mask and gloves. He saw the camera and stared straight at the lens. Judging by the size of the door, I'd say he's at least five foot ten."

"Thanks. That's a big help. More criteria to eliminate some suspects. I'll be down to your office tomorrow morning to view the tape." He ended the call.

"He was here again?" Her voice was wobbly.

"Caught on camera early this morning, dressed in black. And he's at least five ten. That jives with what we saw of the man out at the falls."

She sank down on the couch.

"He's not going to get his hands on you, Tricia. I promise." He scooted across the length of the couch separating them and reached for her.

"Hold me. That's what I need." She snuggled into his arms. "I'm not sure we should have come back here. My bedroom is no longer a safe place after being destroyed so sadistically. The security system doesn't make me feel secure. I don't think I ever told you, but my intuition has been spot on far too many times. Something is going to happen before this is over, something very bad. I feel it."

"Don't. Don't talk like that."

"I can't help it. It's how I feel. Like I'm being submerged in a deep dark lake and I can't get to the surface."

CHAPTER 21

*T*ricia tapped the keys on her office computer, sorting through more pages of the file that she'd transferred from her laptop. Alison had positioned herself between her and the door. Having Alison with her did little to settle her nerves. Fear accompanied her, wherever she was.

The truth was in the pages delivered to her. That's where she'd find the information to save her job. Then a stray thought crept in. If she wanted to save it.

But her first priority was to go over pages of legal documents related to the project. She had trouble concentrating on the facts of a property acquisition when her life was in danger. The clock told her she'd been in the office for over three hours, though it seemed like two days. Nick was picking her up at noon for a quick dash for lunch. They were meeting Doug for an update on the morning's investigation. At least they were including her, keeping her informed of what they were doing.

She focused on the papers in front of her and the computer screen, trying to make time fly more quickly by concentrating on the words on the pages and the rows of numbers on the spreadsheets.

A cell phone rang. She jumped, icy fear skittering down her spine. Alison answered her phone. She was talking to Doug, calling him by name to let her know.

Alison ended the call. "Doug said Nick's SUV has a slashed tire. Doug will pick you up for lunch. You'll stay here with me until he arrives. Someone else will pick up Nick."

Tricia's stomach twisted into a knot. "The guy must have done it. Which means he's not in the building." Or hadn't been earlier. Which was it?

"We can't count on him not sneaking back in. Doug said not to let you out of my sight." Alison shifted her chair closer to Tricia's desk. Tricia closed her files, thoughts of work erased from her mind. They didn't talk about the investigation, in case someone was listening. Alison had been introduced as a temp. Maybe her cover was blown, but they weren't taking chances. After a slashed tire, what came next?

Doug appeared at her door thirty minutes later, leaning on his cane. He greeted her and nodded at Alison. Alison slipped out of the room, to the receptionist desk outside the door.

"Let's go." Doug held the door. "Rafe is picking up Nick from the tire place. Lunch is being delivered to the agency. We'll get you back to work on time."

When they walked into the conference room, Nick, Rafe, and Erik were already there. They had a bunch of pictures spread out on the table. Erik had collected as many pictures as he could of the people on the lists, so they'd have a visual in case something important was revealed in the interview or in the searches.

Tricia scooted a chair over where she could see the pictures. And Nick. Worry lined his face. Her stomach clenched. The guy could be getting desperate. He'd blow soon. And they'd either nab him or he'd do something drastic.

"We've got to get this guy before anyone gets hurt." Doug passed out the box lunches sitting on the table. "He strikes without anyone seeing him or realizing what he's doing."

Tricia lifted her sandwich out of the box and took a bite. Everyone but Erik was eating.

His expression was solemn. "I found a match. Someone to check out further. One of the security guards who works days in the building. Roger Mobley."

"What do you know about him?" Nick set down his sandwich.

"He was in Chicago at the right time, when the last murder happened." Erik shrugged. "Not much to go on, but a start. We need to find out where he worked and what else he did in Chicago and how long he was there. Maybe he has family there."

Tricia's heart rate sped up. "His mother lives in Portland. She used to work for Talbot. We've been friends for years. A very nice woman. She got Roger the job in security."

"Nick, you're quiet. What are you thinking?" Doug asked.

"I met Mobley. He's in the security center on the second floor. His job is monitoring the surveillance cameras installed throughout the building."

Dread spread through Tricia. "He'd have keys and access to the entire building."

Doug pushed his sandwich aside. "He comes to town and his mother gets him a job. Let's check this guy out. I'll call Chet. Nick, you contact security in the building to see if he's working today."

"I hadn't thought of him as a possibility." Tricia held her

sandwich without taking a bite. "His mother is sweet. A lovely woman."

"Have you met Mobley?" Doug asked.

"No, but I think he was in the house one time when I was over there earlier in the year."

"So he knows who you are?"

"I'm sure he does." She searched her memory, wondering where in the house he was while she was in the kitchen with his mother, talking and laughing. "Jane Mobley, his mother, left me a message on my phone last Friday while I was staying at the hotel."

"Do you think he's still living there with her?" Nick asked.

"He could be."

"So, put him at the top of our list," Nick said. "But we can't overlook anyone. Can you think of anyone else we should check on today?" He directed his question to Erik.

"No one else has triggered an alarm for me." Erik appeared thoughtful. "He has access and the right hours. How can we get his DNA?"

"We don't have time," Doug said. "Takes too long to get it processed. In the meantime, he could make his move. We start with his mother."

"Do we have a picture of him?"

Erik rummaged through the stack of pictures and removed the photo of a man around forty years old, with brown hair and a mustache."

"That's him." Nick took the photo.

"Why don't Nick and I go see her?" Rafe asked. "Then I can take him to pick up the SUV. We'll know more after talking to her. I also have three more interviews lined up for this afternoon."

Doug took a sip of coffee and stood. "If anything seems off, call Chet immediately. I have a funny feeling about this man. Too many things are fitting together."

"She's my friend. I should go with you."

Doug shook his head. "No. I'll take you to work, Tricia. You stay there, with Alison. Until this is over."

"Isn't there something I can do?" She felt so helpless.

"You're not trained in investigation. Besides, you're the victim being protected," Doug said. "You've done fine so far. You've given us a lot of information. We have to run with what we have and see what we come up with."

"We need to find out if he's working today," Nick said. "I'd guess not, since my tire was slashed."

"I'll check with security when I take Tricia to work and see if Mobley is there," Doug said. "That will save time."

Nick chuckled. "You're getting more legwork with this case than I bet you've had for a while."

"You're right." He stretched out his crippled right leg. "And I'm feeling more than my normal pain. But this investigation involves family. I can't stay in the office and let my operatives do everything else. I want his guy caught as soon as possible."

"But don't hurt yourself," Nick said.

"I won't. Keeping Tricia safe is top priority."

She saw that look again in Doug's eyes. He really did care.

"THE DRAPES ARE CLOSED." Nick squinted through the rain. "And it's after noon."

"Not a good sign." Rafe parked his SUV in front of the attached garage. A Toyota sat on a paved strip off to the right.

Jane Mobley lived in Tigard, in a small bungalow on a tree-lined street, very typical of neighborhoods in and around Portland.

Nick ignored the light rain and knocked on the door, then rang the doorbell. A gray cat meowed and brushed against his leg. He bent to pet the cat, who meowed again and leaned against the door, wanting in.

No one answered the knock, so they walked around the side of the house to the rear and Rafe peered in a window. "Something's wrong."

"What do you see?" Nick leaned in.

"Take a look." Rafe stepped aside.

Nick took his place at the window. "A shoe in the kitchen doorway. That rug's out of place. The splatter near the rug could be blood."

He reached for his cell phone. "The police need to handle this." He dialed 911. After giving dispatch the information, he called Chet. He was expecting their call. Doug had told him about Mobley and that Nick and Rafe were heading to see Jane Mobley.

Two squad cars from Tigard police arrived with sirens blaring. The officers peered through the window, knocked on the front door, then forced the door, and went inside. Nick and Rafe stayed outside.

A young officer came out, his face pale and haunted. "She's dead. Her throat slashed. Blood splattered in the kitchen."

Nick called Doug. "Bad news. Mobley's mother is dead. Her throat slit."

"And Mobley hasn't been at work since shortly after clocking in this morning. He left immediately, without clocking out. Someone saw him leave."

Nick scowled. "He could be anywhere."

"Did you call Chet?"

"Yes, he's on his way. I hope he contacted the FBI. They need to be in on this too."

"I'll call Thompson, to make sure."

"Are you going to tell Tricia? Or should I?" Nick scrambled into the passenger side of the SUV, out of the rain.

"I'll tell Alison, so she'll be extra alert. You tell Tricia when you get there."

"Do we leave Tricia at work?"

"Yes. Alison is with her. Stop by when you can and tell her about her friend. We'll get her out of there later." Doug ended the call.

The crime scene was cordoned off and the calls made for the fingerprint experts and the medical examiner. Nick and Rafe hung around to give their statements about what they saw and did, then headed for the tire place to pick up Nick's SUV. He hated having to break the news to Tricia about Jane Mobley, but he was the logical one to tell her.

When he walked into her office, Tricia focused on him immediately and stood. A raised brow. Of course she wanted to know what was going on. Alison had been called by Doug.

"Bad news." He shut the office door behind him. Alison remained seated. "Mobley's mother was found on the floor of her kitchen, with her throat slit."

"Oh, no. It couldn't be him! His mother's so nice. Was... Why?" Tricia sank into her chair and put her hands over her face.

Her soft sobs tore at his heart. When he could stand it no longer, he pulled her into his arms and let her cry. The guy had caused so much pain. They had to catch the bastard before he hurt anyone else.

She finally stopped crying and wiped at her tear-stained

face. "Why would he kill his own mother? She was a sweet and loving person." Her words were strained and shaky.

"Okay, two possibilities. He wanted her to help lure you someplace and she refused. In a fit of rage, he killed her. Remember the phone message? Or, he came here planning to kill her too. His mother was a career woman."

"I don't understand how he could do that." Her expression was one of horror. "Could it have been someone else? And this killing is unrelated?"

"No. The police found your red underwear in his bedroom, stuffed in a gym bag. Chet called me when I was on my way here."

"Then there's no doubt. He was the one inside my house. He left those messages. He destroyed my bedroom and my clothes."

"Yes. He was the one." He let go of her.

"I'm sorry he killed her." She dropped into her chair.

"For what it's worth, we have the connection to you."

"I want to talk to Doug, see what he wants me to do to help catch the guy."

"He wants you to stay here with Alison. Mobley's not here. He left the building shortly after clocking in this morning."

She visibly shuddered and clutched her arms to her body. "Unless he sneaked in and is hiding someplace. Or, is planning to come back, to catch me here in the building. Especially if he doesn't expect you to be here."

"You could be right." And he didn't like the feeling that accompanied that thought. "I have to go for a while. I'm meeting with Doug and the FBI and Portland Police in thirty minutes. We'll be coordinating completely. If they decide on a trap here, it can't involve any risk to you. I'll insist on that. And so will Doug."

"No one can guarantee there's no risk." She shook her head. "We don't know what he intends to do or how he plans to do it."

Nick's expression was grim. "At least he's been identified. We know who we're looking for."

"I don't know what he looks like." Alison's words were grim.

Nick took out his cell phone. "I'll have Erik send you a copy." He sent off a message.

"Thanks. That will help."

"If he doesn't disguise himself," Tricia said. "Remember the hooded sweatshirt he's been wearing."

"So we don't leave you alone for a minute." Nick reached for the door handle. "I'll be back as soon as I can. Don't leave this office unless you absolutely have to."

"Okay. You be careful. He's targeted you too. The slashed tire was a warning."

"Or a way to slow me down."

Alison took her gun from her holster and laid it on the top of the desk, and put a piece of paper over it. "Go ahead and go, Nick. I'll watch the door and Tricia." She grimaced. "We'll go armed to the restroom."

CHAPTER 22

The afternoon drug on and the numbers on the spreadsheet didn't make sense, no matter how long Tricia stared at them. They balanced, because the formulas had been altered. And she could find no evidence pointing to who had done the manipulation. Did she even care anymore?

Despite the threats, despite her fears, despite her grief over losing a good friend, she was here with a job to do. Despite the emotions cascading through her.

The problem was her lack of concentration. She couldn't see the possibilities, the solutions to saving this real estate deal. And no one seemed to be making contacts, to raise more money. Their goal was to fix the blame on her for the failure of the project.

Nothing made sense anymore.

Not her job, not her life, not the violence.

She swiveled around in her chair. Alison sat where she had a view out the open door and was within reach of her gun. Two questions nagged at Tricia. When would Mobley strike again? Who else would die?

"I don't want someone else to get hurt because of me." Tricia said the words quietly, so her voice wouldn't carry beyond her office. "He killed his own mother." A tremor raced through her.

"Maybe that was part of his original plan, when he moved in with his mother." Alison's blue eyes were sympathetic. "And if it wasn't you he was targeting, it would have been another woman. Someone without the resources you have. Doug is doing everything humanly possible."

"I realize that. And I feel guilty."

"Don't." Alison checked the hallway outside the door. "Predators like this guy have to be stopped. Better here, instead of him escaping to go somewhere else and target another woman."

"You're right, and that's why I'm here at work." Tricia shifted in her chair. "It feels weird to be involved at this level of violence. I want to wake up and discover it's all been a nightmare."

"Not going to happen until he's caught." Alison's words were emphatic. "And then you'll take years getting over the trauma."

Alison's tone of voice triggered a tightness deep down inside Tricia. "You're talking like you've had experience."

Alison's gaze was full of compassion. "Let's just say I know how you feel." She walked to the door and gazed around the outer office. "People are starting to leave. It's quitting time. Your escorts for the evening should arrive soon."

Alison's change of subject was deliberate. Tricia's curiosity was aroused. She didn't want to talk about her own past. "Escorts as in plural?"

"Doug said two people at least will be with you when you're

moving about. Nick's only one man." She pursed her lips. "I like those odds better."

"I see your point." Tricia swiveled her chair.

"Right on cue. Here come Nick and Kara. I'll wait until you've left the area, then slip out to another elevator and go down to report to the guard in the lobby."

Tricia raised a brow.

"The undercover officer as extra security in the lobby. Chet arranged it."

"You have far more information than I do." Tricia let her frustration ride her words. "When did that start?"

"This afternoon. That's what the call was about. I didn't want to say anything earlier when there were too many people close by."

"I'm sorry. I'm frustrated. I don't want to be kept in the dark. It's my life."

"Okay. I'll remember." Alison flashed that look of compassion again.

She did understand.

Tricia clicked keys on her computer to shut down the file she was using and put her computer into locked sleep mode for the night.

Nick and Kara came through the door. The sight of Nick was reassuring. "Let's go home," he said.

"Hi, Tricia." Kara flicked a strand of dark red hair away from her face. "I hope you don't mind. I'll be at your house tonight, with you and Nick."

Tricia picked up her briefcase. "Of course not." She smiled at Kara, said goodnight to Alison, and followed Nick from the office and through the foyer to the elevator. Kara stayed at her side.

When the elevator door opened at the lobby, people were

shouting. Panic seized Tricia. She froze in place. Nick propelled her through the door into the lobby and positioned himself in front of her. Kara grabbed her arm and steadied her. "What's going on?" Her voice was shaky. "I can't see anything."

"The security guard is trying to get someone out the revolving front door. A patrol car pulled up outside." Nick shifted and Tricia saw the tugging and pushing.

"Let's go." Nick grasped her arm and hustled Tricia over to another door and outside. Rafe had his SUV at the curb and was standing by the open back door. Nick gently guided Tricia into the backseat and slid in beside her, closing the door behind him. Kara got into the front passenger seat. Rafe ran around the car, jumped in, and sped off down the street and around the corner.

Nick's expression was grim. "When we get to your house, I'll check with Chet and find out what happened. In the meantime, I'm staying alert. Rafe has to concentrate on the traffic. Kara is riding shotgun."

That cold chill sped through her and Tricia crouched down in the seat.

TRICIA STAYED low in the seat, her shoulders tensed, her body on alert. Rush hour traffic slowed their progress through downtown and up to her house in the northwest. Rafe let the three of them out in front and waited until Nick had opened the door and they were inside the house before he drove up the street.

Tricia dropped down on the couch. And willed herself to relax.

Kara lingered near the door. "Doug said I should make myself useful. How about a pot of coffee to start with?"

"Thanks. A cup of coffee would help."

Kara headed for the kitchen.

Nick took his laptop from his briefcase and plugged it in. Then opened his cell phone and dialed.

"Chet, did you hear about the scuffle in the lobby of the Talbot building about twenty minutes ago?" A pause. "Thanks. We're inside. She's okay." He ended the call.

"Was it anything?" Tricia didn't like the grim set of Nick's jaw.

"A guy high on meth. Could be random." He set the phone down and powered up his laptop. Then he faced her, a scowl firmly in place. "I realize you're upset about Jane Mobley, but I have to ask you some questions."

"I don't want to think about poor Jane." She blinked at her tears.

"I need information. Or would you rather answer questions for Chet?"

She thought a moment. "Let's get it over with. What do you want to know?" She sighed and tucked her legs up under her, trying to get comfortable.

"When did Mobley show up in town? And how did his mother take his sudden appearance? Did he move right in with her?"

She took another deep breath and let her memory drift through the past few months. "Must have been about May. In the spring, anyway. Jane retired in January and we met for lunch about once a month."

"Did she seem upset when he arrived in town?"

The aroma of brewing coffee wafted from the kitchen. Then Kara walked in carrying two cups. "Black for both of you?"

"Yes." Nick answered.

She set the cups on the coffee table. "I'll go rustle up something for dinner." Her Texas accent embellished her words. "Someone went grocery shopping and left us ready to eat stuff. I'll bring it in when I get everything warmed up." She left the room.

"Thanks," Tricia called after her. She picked up her cup and took a sip, then cradled it in her hands. "Jane seemed distracted when we had lunch. When I asked her if anything was wrong, she said her youngest son had come to town and was staying with her temporarily."

She thought a minute, scrunching her brows as she replayed the scene in her mind. "Then she said she hadn't seen or heard from him in years and didn't understand why he showed up at her house after telling her she'd never see him again. He drove up one day and moved in, without asking if he could."

"Did he ask her to help him get a job?"

"She didn't say. I do know she talked to someone in building management and he ended up getting a security job. I have no idea what kind of work he'd done before."

Nick made notes in his open file, then picked up his coffee and took a sip. His scrunched brows told her he was thinking deeply. Detective work suited him. He was highly intelligent, something she had just begun to realize when they broke up and went their separate ways.

His cell phone rang and he picked it up. "It's Doug." He answered, and listened.

"I'll tell Tricia." He held the phone away from his ear. "Mobley's car was found, a little Honda he bought after coming to town. He could be driving a stolen vehicle. The police are checking out reports of stolen vehicles today, especially any thefts that have happened in the past two or three hours."

"Maybe he's driving his white panel truck."

Nick stared at her. "White panel truck?" He emphasized each word.

"He kept it in his mother's garage, locked up. He told her not to go near it."

"Damn. Doug, Tricia said Mobley had a white panel truck in his mother's garage. He could be driving it."

"What about the truck?" She used her most demanding tone.

"It's where he kills his victims. Doug, I'll call you back." He ended the call and looked at her. Then winched and closed his eyes momentarily, before opening them again.

"Was that what you guys were keeping from me? The fact that the killer drove a white panel truck?"

"Yes." The word came out softly. "For the record, I said you should be told."

Bone deep anger soared through her. "If I'd known about the truck, Jane could be alive today."

CHAPTER 23

A distraught Tricia paced the living room. Nick couldn't think of anything comforting to say. She'd alternated between angry outbursts and quiet tears.

They'd been at the house several hours and she hadn't calmed down. He didn't blame her. He'd be angry too. She was surrounded by people trying to protect her, yet keeping vital information from her. He'd known not telling her everything could have consequences.

She stopped and her stormy gaze locked with his. Would she ever trust him again?

Kara was upstairs napping, since she'd been up early. He was taking first watch. Kara would relieve him at 2:00 am. He hoped Tricia would be able to sleep, if she ever calmed down.

"Come here." He said the words softly.

She shook her head. "No."

"I'll massage some of the stress from your shoulders and neck."

"Not a good idea." She continued her pacing.

He waited until she came close, then intercepted her, folding her into his arms. "Relax a bit. Let me hold you for a few minutes, then I want you to go to bed and go to sleep."

"If you hold me and touch me, I won't be able to sleep." She sank into his embrace, scooting close to his body, as if she were trying to absorb his warmth.

She'd surprised him. "Oh, you shouldn't do that." He groaned. She tilted her head and her lips were so close. He captured her mouth. He'd intended a casual kiss, to distract her. It instantly became much more. She opened to him and he deepened the kiss, dragging her tightly against him. Something ignited within her and her hands roamed his back and up to his hair, as she pressed closer. He broke the kiss. "We can't."

She twisted away, then stumbled. He steadied her.

A muffled bang sounded outside. "Damn." He listened for any other sounds.

"I heard it too. Out in the back."

He ran to the kitchen, tugged the shade aside, and peered into the backyard. Flames jumped into the night sky from the dumpster behind the fence.

"What is it?" Tricia moved to his side.

"Get down." He shoved Tricia to the floor and she scooted to the cabinet and drew herself into a ball. "Scott's out there." He grabbed a phone from the charger in the living room and dialed 911 and told the dispatcher to send the police and fire department immediately. Then he headed to the kitchen. Tricia was huddled on the floor next to the cabinet. She hadn't moved.

"What's going on?" Kara ran into the kitchen, rubbing her sleepy eyes.

"Fire outside in the dumpster. I called the police. Take Tricia upstairs. I don't know where Scott is." Then he called Doug and Chet.

Adrenalin pumped through him. He couldn't check on Scott until the police arrived. Sirens wailed from the street out front. In a matter of minutes a police officer knocked on the door, identifying himself.

"Someone is badly hurt out back. Is it one of yours?" the officer asked.

"Scott Armstrong was outside on watch."

"I've called for an ambulance. He has a head wound gushing blood."

One officer stayed by the open door while Nick followed the first officer around the house. In the dim shadows, Nick could make out a prone man on the grass, another officer bending over him, applying pressure to the gash on the back of his head. Scott moaned. He was alive.

A blaring siren announced the arrival of the ambulance. Scott was placed on a gurney and whisked off to the hospital.

When Nick came back inside, Chet had arrived and was talking to Tricia in the living room. "We have to stop him as quickly as we can," Tricia said. "before someone else gets hurt. How can we set a trap for him?"

"No. I won't use you for bait." Doug walked in the door.

Tricia swiveled around at the sound of Doug's voice. "I'm tired of this nonsense. I can't live a normal life." She blew out an exasperated breath. "Scott is injured and I've lost a good friend. Jane Mobley. He has to be caught and put in prison." She sank onto the couch.

Nick took the other end of the couch. "He likes fire. He's used it twice. In the hotel and here. We have to stop him from doing something drastic downtown in the office building."

"How?" Chet sat in one chair. "Do you have an idea?"

Doug took the other chair.

"This guy is getting desperate, and beyond rational," Nick

said. "He's going to get careless. I say we should be ready with saturation patrols in the building tomorrow. He might go for her there by creating another diversion, since this one didn't work."

"I'll call the chief and have SERT on standby, with their extra fire power," Chet said. "I'll also alert the fire department. If Mobley tries anything, we'll get him tomorrow."

"And I go to work and act as if nothing has happened." Tricia bounced up from the couch. "When will this nightmare end?"

TRICIA WOKE in the middle of the night to the sound of gentle snoring and a weight at her side.

And that oh so alluring scent of Nick. His male essence she loved.

He'd fallen asleep on her bed, talking to her, helping her calm down and go to sleep.

His breathing caused a gentle rise and fall of his chest under the sweater he wore. She wanted him. But giving in to passion was too dangerous. They had to stay alert to any strange sounds.

Kara was asleep on the couch in the living room. The police were patrolling the neighborhood for the rest of the night. And they'd be out there until Mobley was captured. Even the police were on high alert.

Nick had planned to stay on the couch and watch down there, but Kara said she would, since she'd already had a couple hours of sleep before the commotion woke her up. So Nick came in here with her and they'd both fallen asleep from sheer exhaustion.

She needed to go back to sleep to be ready for another

stress-filled day. Maybe it would end tomorrow. Today. It was well after midnight.

She shifted to her side where she could see him better. The dim glow from the night light cast shadows on his face.

She eased back and he stirred, his eyes opening and gazing directly into hers. "Can't you sleep?" His voice was husky.

"I woke up. I heard snoring. You said you were going to sleep in the other bed tonight."

"I was. I got sidetracked. I'm glad I did." He reached for her and nestled her head under his chin. "I want to hold you, so I know you're safe."

"Having you here makes me feel safe." She lifted her head and gazed into the darkness of his eyes.

His mouth came down on hers, gently, softly, persuasively, until she opened to him. He deepened the kiss—and she was no longer safe. That was exactly what they were doing last night when the fire started. Not a good idea.

Yet she kissed him back, pouring her pent up desires into the kiss. Her hands began to roam his sweater, up to his nape. She pressed against him, wanting so much more. When he kissed her, she doubted her desire for independence. Doubted she could stay immune to him. Doubted she truly wanted to be alone. She'd discovered he was everything she wanted in a man.

Nothing was clear to her anymore. Not after Nick came to town and completely overturned her already complicated life.

He raised his head. "I lost control." He rolled off the bed. "I'll go to the other room and let you sleep. So I can sleep too." He closed the door behind him.

A strange emptiness settled in her midsection. No, she didn't need Nick. Couldn't need Nick. Her mother had been a prisoner of her own needs for too many years.

She'd have to let Nick go when this was over. And it would be over soon. Her intuition told her that.

But letting Nick go would be the hardest thing she ever did. Even harder than when she ran off to law school so many years ago. She'd fallen completely in love with Nick Castellani.

CHAPTER 24

$\mathcal{T}$ricia reviewed the figures on the spreadsheet once again. As if she would find something different. Today was her last chance to save her job, the deadline Talbot had given her. The email he'd sent her on Tuesday, when she'd returned to work, stated specifically that she had until noon on Thursday. Her last extension. Today was Thursday.

Knots in her chest and stomach coiled tighter with each minute that passed. Yet she also felt deep down inside today would be the day Mobley would do whatever he planned to do.

She fought the urge to call Nick and tell him to come get her.

Alison sat in a chair behind her, watching the door. Making no attempt to appear busy. A newspaper hid her gun. Kara was out at the reception desk, not far from her office door.

Despite her promise to herself to save her job, everything she'd compiled on the hotel project didn't make sense. The missing bid meant Talbot didn't have enough financing. So far he hadn't responded to the email she'd sent Tuesday morning. Her job was to figure out why the real estate deal was collapsing. And try to get her boss to listen to her concerns about the spreadsheet being altered. He'd demanded the final figures today.

And that's why a portion of her thoughts were on her work, the work that had sustained her for such a long time. The work she thought she loved.

She'd begun questioning her choices. The way she'd shut Nick out ten years ago because she didn't want to ever need a man like her mother had needed her father. The way she shut out the possibility there could be more to life than an education and a job.

Life without Nick would be cold and dreary, like the Northwest winters. She was beginning to see possibilities she hadn't seen before.

But first Mobley had to be stopped before he killed anyone else. She shuddered. He'd killed his own mother. What kind of monster could do that? She stared at the monitor in front of her and her eyes filled with unshed tears, blocking out the figures on the screen.

Several minutes later Nick sauntered into her office, and her emotions subtly shifted. She never tired of gazing at him. He was classically handsome, but in his own rugged way. The dark depths of his intensely perceptive eyes saw more than she wanted him to see.

He dropped into a chair in front of her desk. "I'm going to cruise the building with a supervisor from building management. We're looking for any indication he's going to try something here." He kept his voice low, in case someone was passing by the office.

"Be careful. He's after you too."

"Yeah." He grinned at her and flipped open his jacket to reveal his shoulder holster."

"Remember, he hits people over the head," Alison said. "From behind. Scott's still in the hospital."

A guilt pang slammed Tricia. "Any more word about his condition?"

Alison swiveled in her chair. "Doug said this morning he's doing as fine as can be expected, but he'll need time to heal. He had over a dozen stitches in his scalp. And a concussion."

Nick stood and pushed the chair out of the way. "No one is going anywhere alone anymore. Doug issued the order as soon as Scott was attacked."

He scowled, his eyes dark, then gripped the door jamb. "I'll be back in time to take you to lunch." He disappeared from view.

She stared at the empty doorway. He was far too much of a distraction. Maybe he'd find something and catch the guy. Without getting hurt himself. Conflicting emotions raced through her. She tugged her attention to the screen.

The phone rang. Dread raced through her. She picked up the receiver. Her boss's secretary summoned her to the conference room for an emergency meeting.

What was the emergency? Finding another way to blame her. She'd have to go to hear what he had to say. The receptionist said Mr. Talbot wanted her legal opinion and wanted her to verify some facts. She rechecked the figures she'd been trying to make balance. Maybe he'd listen to her today when she told him the proposed deal didn't have a chance without more financing. Or maybe he didn't care what she said.

Tricia printed out the file on the screen. "Let's go. I'm needed in the conference room down the hall."

Alison put her gun in her belt holster and adjusted her

jacket to hide it. Tricia added the new sheet to her file folder and picked it up from the desk.

She stopped in front of Kara. "We're going down the hall to the conference room. Tell Nick when you see him."

"I'll keep a watch here, for Mobley or anything else suspicious."

"We shouldn't be long."

She and Alison headed down the hall. There were so many things to consider every time she left her office. She brushed at her temple where a tension headache had begun.

Even though the meeting was vitally important, Tricia didn't feel safe going someplace Nick didn't know about. Kara could tell him, but she also worried about him. He was the one touring the building. He was the one who could surprise Mobley. He was the one who could be Mobley's next target, since he spent the nights in her house.

Coming back here had not been a good idea. Too late. She'd have to play out this charade.

Tricia settled into a chair at the conference table and spread out her notes and files. Alison sat in the corner of the room facing the door. Norm Talbot paced impatiently as everyone gathered. Occasionally he would glance her direction with a scowl. The knot that had been in Tricia's stomach earlier tightened into a solid ball.

The door closed behind the last person. Eight people had been called to this emergency meeting, including the chief financial officer of the company. Randolph Parker. The man Tricia suspected was behind the missing bid. Not that he would ever admit it.

Norm Talbot wasn't a big man but he wielded his power like a club. He wasn't much older than Tricia, maybe by five or so years. His father had enticed him to join the firm about three years earlier with the promise of a vice presidency. He'd get that promotion any way he could.

Talbot strode to the end of the table and instead of taking a seat, he stood behind his chair. The knot in her stomach ached.

"Ms. Landreth." He stared at her, along with everyone else at the table. "You have caused too many distractions. If this deal fails, it will be your fault."

She matched his stare. She had an explanation, but he wouldn't care. He'd made his decision. "Mr. Talbot, the figures don't balance because there's a bid missing from the original financial package. I've gone over and over the data. You don't have enough financing in place now to complete the project." She kept her voice as steady as she could, not willing to show any sign of weakness.

"What do you mean?"

"Exactly what I said. You don't have adequate financing. One of the investors dropped out of the deal last week and no other arrangements were made to make up for the loss." She stared at Parker, but he deliberately avoided eye contact.

"Why wasn't I informed?"

"You were. By email memo Tuesday morning." Despite the nervous energy cascading through her, she kept her voice steady. "I discovered the missing bid in a pile of documents the finance office loaned me to look through. I scanned them and found the bid on Sunday when I was without cell and internet connections."

"That was your fault."

"Did you get the email memo I sent you Tuesday morning?"

"No. You didn't send it."

Her chest constricted, making her breathing shallow. He was calling her a liar. He'd made up his mind that she was the problem, that she was expendable.

"Yes, I did send it." She maintained eye contact. He was the one who flinched first. "I've done my job. I've filed the necessary documents. I've vetted the figures. Checked the legal angles. But one investor withdrew. The figures were manipulated to hide that fact. I was never informed. Someone altered the formulas on the spreadsheet."

"That's not true. You didn't do your job properly." He rounded the table and shoved a paper in front of her. "Go back to your office and work through this itemized list of instructions. Make the figures fit."

Talbot then sat in the chair at the end of the table and asked for input from three other people. They didn't add anything significant to the discussion. No one would stand up for her. They valued their own jobs over principles. The failure of this project meant the end of her job here. Far too much was riding on this one deal. Talbot blamed her. Not the real culprit, whoever that was.

Talbot stood. "Ms. Landreth, you have one hour to figure out where you've misstated the figures." He strode from the room.

NICK ACCOMPANIED BILL SHIFFRON, from building management, around the corner on the twelfth floor. They stopped to observe the construction crews renovating the office space for a new firm to move in. Workers were measuring and cutting boards in the open hallway. Others were working inside office spaces. Everyone seemed on task, which meant nobody extra had infiltrated. Though Nick assumed Mobley worked alone, they wasn't taking chances. Mobley might pay someone to cause a distraction that would benefit him.

They checked out the stairway the construction crew used when not using the freight elevator at the back of the building. No security in sight. Anyone could come and go at will, up from the ground floor. Nick muttered a curse. "Someone should be guarding this staircase. SERT better be on the job at the ground level."

"I'll call security and get someone up here." Shiffron took his phone from his belt.

"Some SERT members should be inside too." Nick took out his cell phone and punched in Chet's number.

Chet answered immediately.

"Is SERT watching the perimeter of the building?"

"They've been in place since Tricia arrived."

"Could someone be assigned to the construction area on the twelfth floor? Lots of workers coming and going, using a back staircase and a freight elevator."

"I'll see to it. My one concern is that SERT wasn't in place early enough. We don't know if Mobley is in the building or not."

"Damn. He could have come in early. We need to stay alert for signs that he's here."

"I'm almost there. I'll check in with you when I arrive." Chet ended the call.

"Hal Roesch is on his way here," Shiffron said. "He's leaving the new guy on the desk by the front door. I'll call in extra security staff for overtime until this is resolved."

"Thanks." Nick took a last look at the wide-open staircase. "I'm going back to Tricia."

"I'll stay here until Hal arrives. Then I'll come back, in case you need something else."

Nick hesitated a moment, then ran down the hall to the interior staircase, his adrenaline rushing. He'd told Tricia he wouldn't be alone, but that couldn't be helped. Something was happening. He had that prickly feeling on the nape of his neck.

When he reached Tricia's office, Kara was at the outside desk. His heart pounded in his chest after his run down four flights of stairs. He checked the office. No Tricia or Alison. "Where is she?" His anger rose. He stifled a curse.

"She was called to an emergency meeting in the conference room. Alison is with her. I'm on duty here."

"That's not according to the plan for the morning." Nick scowled. "Even Talbot had been informed by the police."

Kara shrugged. "Business types forget everything when deals and money are involved. Tricia is upset over whatever she's working on. Her boss is pressuring her."

"The hell with the deal."

"She's not alone. She's right down the hall. Anyone going that way passes by this desk."

"Not good enough." Nick sat down inside the office, though he couldn't relax. He'd give her ten minutes, then he'd go find her. What he wanted to do was get her out of the building before Mobley made his play.

Five minutes later he heard voices coming down the corridor. He jumped up and looked out the door. They were coming. He relaxed yet stayed alert.

Their eyes met when she came through the door. "You weren't supposed to leave this office." His words accused.

"I was doing my job." She brushed by him to sit down at her desk. She opened a file on the computer and typed in notes about the meeting, about what Talbot said.

"We need to get you out of the building," Nick hovered behind her. "SERT didn't get here until you did. Mobley could have come in earlier." He glanced at the clock on the wall. Almost eleven. "Let's go to lunch."

Fear flashed in her eyes. "I can't leave. I have one hour to figure out how to save the deal. And my job."

"What's with Talbot?"

"He wants this convention hotel. You've seen how hard I've been working on it. Keeping my job depends on figuring out what went wrong. I have to try. I have to rework the figures once more and deliver the results to him within an hour."

"You're crazy. You'd jeopardize your life for your job?"

"I won't give up without a fight. Sit down, or go out in the hallway. I have work to do." She picked up the piece of paper in front of her. Alison scooted her chair into the corner where she faced the door.

"You'd better be fast. You don't have much time."

"I told you, one hour, then I'll go."

"No." He stomped out the door, closing it behind him.

Tricia stared at the door. One last chance. She swiveled to the computer.

CHAPTER 25

Thirty tense minutes later Tricia threw Talbot's list of instructions down on the desk. He was crazy if he thought his silly ideas would work. Busy work. Something to keep her distracted. If the money wasn't there, it wasn't there. Period. Okay, he didn't want her to succeed. Why?

So he could blame the project failure on her? Then he wouldn't be a failure in his father's eyes? Was his ego that fragile? Maybe so.

She picked up the phone to call one of her contacts at another company, and ended the call as frustrated as before. One more chance. She dialed another number. No help there either. The minutes ticked slowly by. When her phone rang, her time would be up. And she had no answers for Talbot.

Nick's cell phone rang behind her. She tensed. He'd come back into her office while she was concentrating. He answered the call and listened. She couldn't hear the other end of the conversation but Nick didn't like what he heard. He was steaming mad and cursing.

He ended the call, and his angry eyes glared at her. "Hal Roesch was found on the back staircase, his head bashed in. He's dead."

Her stomach twisted into a screeching knot of guilt. Hal dead. No. She lurched to her feet. "It's my fault."

"Mobley's in the building. We have to get you out of here." Nick's voice was insistent.

The knot twisted tighter. "Can't you flush him out? He has to be stopped before someone else dies." Panic built inside her. She gulped a breath.

"No. We can't risk it. You have to leave. He's familiar with this entire building."

She looked hard at Nick. And made a decision. "Just a few more minutes, then I'll leave with you."

"Make it quick. Doug and Chet are downstairs. I'll be outside your door."

She sat at her computer, opened her word processor, and began typing. The words came easily. She should have done this last week, before anyone was hurt or killed. Another twist of the knot doubled the pain in her stomach. She printed out the page and signed the bottom. Then she scanned the document and emailed a copy to Human Resources.

She picked up the page with a satisfied scowl and reread it. Nick was talking to Kara. It no longer mattered that Kara and Alison were pegged as bodyguards by her co-workers. Everyone on the floor was aware of what was going on. Rumors were flying and the truth came out. They wanted everyone watching for Mobley, in case he was roaming the halls some-where. His picture had been circulated widely since early that morning.

Nick's cell phone rang again. His raised voice told her he was upset.

He poked his head through the door. "I have to go check on something. Stay here."

"I'll be here or down the hall in Talbot's office."

His expression was one of exasperation. "Alison, watch her closely."

"I am, Nick."

He disappeared from view and a flash of relief raced through her. Too much happening. Too fast. Too complicated.

Her desk phone rang. She stared at it for a few seconds, then picked up the receiver. "Tricia Landreth."

"Report to Norm Talbot's office immediately."

Tricia lowered the phone slowly, an emptiness inside. This was it. She took a big breath and stood.

"You okay?" Alison rose and pushed the chair to the side.

"I don't have the answers he wanted. The miracle. But it doesn't matter anymore."

She took another bracing breath and picked up her papers and files, out of habit. Not because there was new information there. The deal was dead unless Talbot found additional investment funds. And he'd summoned her to his office, rather than the conference room. His mind was made up.

Out of habit, she picked up her cell phone and put it into her jacket pocket.

They passed the conference room, then rounded the corner into the executive corridor. Alison at her side said nothing. Tricia hadn't told her what she was doing.

"I'll stay by the door so I can see down the hallway." Alison stopped at the outer door to Talbot's office.

"Thanks." Tricia went through the open door.

"He's expecting you. Go on in," the receptionist said.

Tricia pushed open the inner door, the knot in her stomach twisting tighter.

Talbot sat behind his big desk. "Did you find your mistakes? Did you make the financing work?" His tone was combative.

She walked to the center of the room and stopped in front of his desk, taking her time, collecting her thoughts. He remained seated.

"The acquisition won't work with the financing currently in place. I told you that earlier." When he didn't say anything, she continued. "I've contacted two additional sources who say the same. There was a cover-up in the finance department when the bid was withdrawn. The deal had no chance without more financing. No amount of legal manipulation is going to make a difference." She paused and waited for Talbot's reaction.

"You should have caught it."

"I was not given the correct figures by the finance department until last Thursday. Then they loaned me a thick document file I sorted through to find the truth."

"Blame someone else." The steeliness of his words cut through her.

And goaded her to continue. "I'm not the one who screwed up. You're covering for your friend Parker. I should have figured that out earlier."

"You're fired." He stood and came around the desk, stopping in front of her.

"You're a little late. I've already faxed my resignation to Human Resources. I can't work for you. You've used me as a scapegoat to protect your cronies in the Finance Department. And to protect yourself from blame. You were well aware I couldn't save the deal." She picked up the letter from the top of the pile in her arms and handed it to Talbot. "Here's your copy of my resignation, complete with the reasons why I can't work for you any longer."

He scanned the page. "These are lies."

Her stomach churned. "No. They're not." She said the words as calmly as she could.

"If you hadn't been so distracted by your personal problems, you could have caught the error sooner."

"My personal problems, as you call them, have been caused by an employee of this building. A member of the security department has been stalking and threatening me."

"You don't have proof."

"Yes I do. And so do the police."

"No excuses. Go clean out your office and leave the premises as soon as you can get out the door."

"I intend to." She held her head high and walked out of the office.

The roiling in her stomach increased. She'd held her temper in check, though she had wanted to shout at him, curse at him. Seven years she'd worked for Talbot Enterprises. Seven years she'd devoted her life to her career. To have her job end like this. Maybe because she hadn't been on top of things and hadn't caught the error sooner. Yes, it could have been her fault. She shouldn't have been so distracted, but it hurt anyway. Deep, deep down. Her career was her life. At least her dignity was intact.

Back in the hallway, close to tears, Tricia looked for Alison. She was nowhere in the hallway. And no one else was in sight. She pulled her cell phone out of her pocket and called Nick. He didn't answer. Next she tried Kara.

"Is something wrong?" Kara asked.

"Yes. I don't know where Alison is. I need to stop at the restroom. I don't dare wait any longer. Nick didn't answer his phone. See if you can get through to him. I'll be right back."

She tossed the papers and files she was carrying into the first trash can she came to. Then stopped outside the restroom.

Mobley was in the building. She pushed open the door and looked around. She bent down. No feet visible. She pushed open the door of each stall. No sounds. She was alone.

She'd get out of the building as fast as she could. And leave town. Let the police catch the killer. Catch Roger Mobley. A monster.

TRICIA SHOVED the door of the stall open a few minutes later. Roger Mobley stood in front of her, a gun pointed at her head.

Her heart faltered, then did a fast restart that quickly skyrocketed to high speed pounding. She couldn't argue with a madman. Or a gun.

"Don't make a sound, bitch." His dark eyes were dilated, like he was in a frenzy. He'd shaved off his mustache and was wearing the same black hooded sweatshirt. The stench of stale cigarette smoke clung to him.

Terror seized her, paralyzing her throat, rendering her incapable of speech or a scream. The adrenaline pouring through her kept her from collapsing. Where was Alison? Nick?

"Turn around." He said the words with that menacing growl familiar from the telephone messages.

Tricia pivoted slowly, bracing for a blow to her head. Instead, Mobley grabbed her wrists and twisted her arms behind her. Pain exploded in her shoulders and shot down her arms. He secured her hands with plastic ties, wrenching them tight. They dug into her flesh and burned like she'd been scalded. She opened her mouth to scream, but bit it back. Then he wrapped a scarf around her mouth, and her chance to scream was gone.

She gagged, nausea choking her. She managed to swallow it

down, but it left a sour taste in her mouth. If she kept her wits about her she might survive.

He shoved her through a rear door of the restroom, into a concrete corridor, and locked the door with a key from the ring hanging from his belt. She'd used that restroom for years, yet never questioned where the door led. Would Alison and Nick find her in time? A knot of fear settled in the pit of her stomach.

Mobley grabbed her arm, propelling her down a concrete hallway toward a stairway door standing open. She stumbled and he jerked her upright. Pain stabbed her shoulder. She kicked off her high heels. Breaking an ankle wouldn't help her. She had no way to stop him from taking her down those stairs. But she could slow him down and give someone time to figure out she was missing and where he'd taken her.

Her body throbbed with sheer panic. Her chest tightened until she thought her ribs would crush her lungs. Sheer will kept her upright. And Mobley's iron grip.

He pushed her through the door into the stairwell. The door clanged shut behind her. He reached around and locked it with a key from the same ring on his belt. The adrenalin rush in her body accelerated. Another barrier blocked help from getting to her.

The dim light in the stairwell did not obscure the cold, hard expression on Mobley's face. The determination. And the barrel of the gun pointed at her head. His left hand bit into her arm. "Down those stairs." His words were harsh, guttural.

What would happen at the bottom of the stairs? Survival meant outwitting him. Or was this the day she would die?

NICK ROUNDED the corner at a run. Kara was rushing toward him, down the hallway. "Where's Tricia?" He shouted at Kara.

"She hasn't come back from the restroom and there's no one in there. And Alison is missing."

"Go look again. I'll be right there."

Kara reversed direction and headed back down the hallway.

Nick flipped open his phone and dialed Chet's number. Chet answered immediately.

"Where are you?"

"In front of the building. Checking with the SERT officers."

"Mobley's white panel truck is parked at the rear door of the basement, hidden under a tarp. I'm getting Tricia out of here as soon as I find her. She went to her boss's office."

"I'll get them deployed inside as well as outside." He ended the call.

Nick met an agitated Kara in the hallway.

"No Tricia and no Alison. Someone saw Tricia go into the restroom, but she's not there. No one saw her come out. A Human Resources clerk was waiting for her, to escort her from the building. They tried to fire her, but she'd already resigned."

"You're sure?" Nick almost shouted.

"That's what the clerk said."

"Damn. No wonder she ran off by herself." Nick could only guess at her state of mind.

Bill Shiffron and Alison came running down the hall. "I found her tied up in a storage room. I heard her kicking the door." He was breathless from his sprint.

Alison seemed to be okay.

"What happened?"

"Mobley pointed a gun at me, then grabbed my arms." Alison gulped a breath. "He's probably got Tricia. She's not in Talbot's office."

"She went into the restroom, but she's not there," Kara said.

"He could have taken her out the back door of the restroom," Shiffron said. "He'd have keys to the service corridors. That's why we haven't seen him." He took a set of keys out of his pocket.

"His truck is outside the basement door. How will he get her down there?"

"Probably the staircase that goes to the basement, or the elevator. Come, I'll open the door for you."

"Let's go." Nick's heart constricted. Despite their precautions, he'd gotten to her anyway. But Mobley wasn't going to get her out of the building. The building was essentially locked down with SERT here. But he couldn't count on them. He'd find Mobley before he hurt Tricia. He'd never be able to live with himself if he couldn't save her from that demon.

He followed Shiffron through the restroom and out the back door. His heart slammed into overdrive. "There's her shoes, near the stairway door. Mobley is taking her down the stairs." Panic laced his voice.

"Go that way, to the elevator." Shiffron handed him a set of keys. "Here's the key to activate it."

"Tell Chet and Doug I'm heading for the basement. And to send SERT." Nick sprinted down the corridor, heading to the elevator.

CHAPTER 26

Tricia's right shoulder throbbed with pain and burned like it was coming out of its socket. Mobley's grip on her arm tightened with each step as he dragged her down the stairs. Sharp pain radiated down her arm and across her shoulders. She held back as much as she could, to slow him down. In retaliation, he twisted her arm as he pulled and pushed at her.

Her foot tripped on the concrete step and her knees buckled. Mobley yanked her upright. "Keep going. Fast." He bellowed the words and yanked harder on her arm. The gun in his right hand pointed directly at her head.

Stark terror gripped her. The abrasive concrete of the stairs ripped her stockings and cut the bottoms of her feet. The blood from the cuts made the steps slippery and that much harder to go down at the pace Mobley was pushing her. Her balance was off and she was woozy with pain, and unstable. But staying upright meant a better chance at surviving. She couldn't risk angering him too much.

Where was Alison? For a moment, fear for what happened

to her took over. If he'd killed Alison, and she survived, she wouldn't be able to live with her guilt. People were dying because of her. And she couldn't help them.

She'd lost count of how many flights of stairs they'd gone down.

"Come on, bitch. Hurry. You've caused me too much trouble. I'm going to enjoy watching you die real slow. When I'm through with you." He growled out the words and tugged harder on her arm.

Two more flights of stairs. Her head spun, making her feel faint, but she fought to stay conscious. Where was he taking her? Probably had his truck by an outside door. He couldn't get her out of the building, could he? What chance did she have?

The last door they passed had a number two on it. Almost down to ground level. They kept going, even further. To the basement?

He shoved open the heavy door at the bottom of the stairwell. He didn't bother to lock this one. Her hope plummeted.

They were indeed in a basement. A dark one. The air reeked of the oily smell of machinery. A steady hum came from an electrical panel. Pipes and wiring and machines of various sizes were scattered about. A warren of corridors provided places where Mobley could hide if someone came in. Her stomach knotted tighter as despair took over. He pushed her through a narrow passage into another room where more electrical equipment lined the walls.

Then he stopped and jammed the gun to her head. The gun barrel struck her temple and sent a shooting pain through her skull. "You're a cold bitch, like my mother. You have to die. But not yet. I have plans for you first." He stared at her with pure hatred in his eyes. She tried to stare at him with the same intensity. Not let him see how scared she was.

He pushed her toward a door at the rear of the room. Did it lead to the outside? The gag was choking her, bringing back the nausea. She concentrated on not vomiting. *Breathe slowly. Stay calm. Wait for your chance.*

A noise behind her. She flinched. Was someone else in the basement? Nick? The police? Mobley heard it too, and rammed the gun against her head so hard she felt a bruise forming. He tightened the hold on her arm and twisted it harder to keep control. She had no choice but to go where he led.

She caught a glimpse of Nick behind a machine near the wall. He was crouched down so only the top of his head showed. The waves in his dark hair shone in the dull light.

Mobley was holding her in front of him. He must have sensed that someone was there too. He was alert and watching, while moving steadily toward a door leading to the outside. Light shone through a small window above the door. Is this where she would die? Or in his truck? Bleeding to death?

The barrel of Nick's gun glinted in the semi darkness of the basement. They would have to cross an open area to reach the door.

"Stay where you are or I put a bullet in her head." Mobley shouted over the hum of the machines.

Steely resolve took over. Staying on this side of the door gave her the best chance of survival. And she couldn't let Nick risk his life trying to save her. She didn't want him to die.

"Hold still, bitch." Mobley pushed the barrel of the gun tighter against her temple.

She let her legs buckle under her, as if she were fainting, and dropped to the side, pulling Mobley with her. The gun dislodged from her head. Two shots rang out. The right side of her head stung. Then darkness blotted out all light.

~

NICK'S HEART ALMOST STOPPED. Tricia fell to the concrete, blood gushing from a wound on the side of her head. Panic gripped him. He looked for Mobley. On the floor too. Not moving.

Nick gripped his gun tighter and dodged around the machinery. He rushed to where Tricia lay in a crumpled heap. His heart was in his throat. Her head had been grazed by the bullet from Mobley's gun and she was unconscious, but the slug hadn't gone into her skull. Mobley took a head shot and blood pooled under him. If he wasn't dead yet, he would be soon. Nick kicked Mobley's gun several feet to the side.

Then he carefully removed the gag from around Tricia's mouth. She gulped for air and moaned. She was still alive. He cut off the plastic restraints on her wrists with his pocket knife and laid her out on the concrete. He stripped off his shirts and put the heavier one under her head and used his T-shirt to apply pressure to her wound, to slow the flow of blood. Then he heard footsteps running his direction. Someone else had come down the elevator.

Bill Shiffron rounded the corner and stopped. "I heard shots."

"Mobley's down. I hope he's dead." Nick motioned toward the door. "Open the outer door and summon an ambulance. There should be one standing by."

Three SERT members ran through the opened door. Then Chet and Doug.

Doug rushed to his side and knelt down to look at Tricia. "She's breathing."

"The bullet from Mobley's gun grazed the side of her head. She's going to have one whopping headache."

Doug looked up. "Your shot got Mobley?"

"Yes. No other choice. He was behind her and had the gun barrel jammed to her temple. She pulled him off balance so I could get a clear shot at his head. Not the best shot to take, but all I had in that split second."

"One gutsy young woman." Pride shown in Doug's voice as he used his cane to get back up. And the relief that the manhunt was over with Mobley the one dead.

"The ambulance is coming around the building." Chet stopped to check Mobley. "No pulse." He glanced at Tricia. "How's she doing?"

Nick looked up. "Unconscious but breathing."

A burst from the siren outside signaled the arrival of the ambulance. The crew came in, tended to Tricia's wound, then loaded her onto a gurney.

Nick grabbed the shirt that had been under her head and put it back on, despite the blood staining it.

"Go with her," Chet said. "I'll get your statement later. You did what you had to do."

"Thanks." Nick followed the gurney out the door. As soon as he was outside the building, his arms and legs began to shake. He'd come so close to losing her. Not that she was truly his. Not yet.

EVEN THE SOFTEST chair felt like a brick bench after several hours. But Nick would not leave the waiting room until he'd seen Tricia and knew she was all right.

She'd been unconscious after she was hit, unconscious during the ride in the ambulance, unconscious when they wheeled her down to the trauma center.

The door opened and Doug limped in, using his cane to

support his weight. He released the door and it banged shut behind him. He dropped into the closest chair and let the cane fall to the floor. His face was drawn and haggard.

"Did you stop at the desk? Did they tell you anything?"

Doug slouched in the chair. "The duty nurse said the doctor would come in and brief us, as soon as she's completely stable. There was a small complication." His voice lacked its usual forcefulness.

Bands of tension tightened around Nick's chest. "Complication?"

"Something to do with her blood pressure, but she's okay now. And they've stitched her up, though she's still unconscious. She's heavily sedated."

Nick willed his body to relax. "She's going to be in pain for a while. That was a nasty gash."

"But she's alive." The relief came through in Doug's tone. "And I was wrong about keeping details from Tricia. The white panel truck."

"We both made mistakes. The picture of us kissing at the falls."

"But she's alive," he repeated. "Thank you for saving her from that psychopath." Doug's words were sincere.

Coming from Doug, that was high praise. "But I shot and killed another human being."

"You had no choice, given the circumstances. He was less than human. We underestimated him."

"Can a guy be a good cop while killing the sorry bastards?" Another question he had to ask.

"It's weighing on your mind. The two hoods down in L.A. Then Mobley. But you're a good cop. Believe that." More sincere words from Doug.

"I thought you'd decided I didn't know what I was doing." Nick stood and stretched his cramped muscles.

"A bodyguard isn't supposed to fall in love with the person he's protecting." No anger in Doug's tone. That surprised him.

"Why did you give me the job?" He needed the answer. Yet he'd dreaded asking Doug directly.

"Because I knew you'd protect her completely. Because you're good at what you do. Because of your past relationship with her."

"You set me up."

"I guess I did. I thought your job in Los Angeles would keep you from falling for her." Doug's eyebrows raised, a questioning gesture. He was wondering why.

So was Nick. He'd fallen completely in love with her.

Nick peered through the little window of the door at the almost vacant hallway. "I'm going to tell you something, but I want you to promise you won't tell Tricia."

"Okay."

"I quit my job on Monday. The lieutenant called and ordered me back to work Tuesday morning. He wouldn't let me have any more time."

"Were you and he having a problem?"

"Let's just say I've worked under better lieutenants than he was."

"I see. And you want to tell Tricia yourself? When?"

"When I've figured out the right timing." He plopped into the chair where he'd been sitting. "We have things to work out first."

"So you two haven't resolved what broke up your relationship years ago." A statement. Not a question.

"Far from it. Like I said. We have things to work out."

"You quit your job, even though you hadn't any idea if she'd want you to stay." Another statement.

"I had no choice. I couldn't fly back to L.A. when she was in danger."

"I'm sorry bringing you up here cost you the job you loved." He cleared his throat. "We're even. You don't owe me anything."

"Are we?"

"Definitely. Besides, I never blamed you for the bomb blast. I doubt you could have done anything to stop it. And it wasn't your fault you'd been awake for over thirty-six hours. That nap probably saved your own life."

Nick thought a moment, trying to understand. "Why?"

"If you'd made it to the restaurant that night, you might have been near the car too. I'd have lost a friend as well as my wife."

Nick hesitated. The swell of emotion inside him had him in a choke hold. He'd held onto the guilt for years, beating himself up for falling asleep when his friend was in danger. Could he let it go?

"Why did we have that argument four years ago? Before you moved to Portland?" Another question he needed an answer to.

"Because I was lashing out at anyone and everyone in those days, feeling sorry for myself. With the passage of time, I'm thinking more clearly. I made several enemies that last year."

"I never considered you an enemy. But I'm glad you cleared up one question for me. That you don't blame me."

"I never truly blamed you. And I'm sorry I acted like such a damn fool."

"Apology accepted." Nick heaved a big sigh. "That helps me make a decision I've been mulling over."

"About staying here?"

"Yes. Chet hinted there might be a place for me locally."

"I hope you take it. And I hope Tricia doesn't make you want to leave."

"You won't care if we do end up together?"

"No. And that's the honest truth." Doug shifted in the chair and Nick could tell he was hurting.

"Tricia doesn't trust a man to be there for her. Like her dad wasn't there for her or her mother."

"I hope my daughters haven't grown up believing you can't trust a man because I'm not in their lives." Doug frowned and shook his head, as if the idea was new to him.

"A little different situation."

"Maybe so. Is that why Tricia doesn't particularly like me, had distanced herself from me? Because I don't see my daughters?"

"You'll have to ask her that. She didn't say anything to me about your daughters. She talked about her father and her mother."

"Did you know Moreno is the reason Jenny left and took Dani and Lindi?"

"Someone told me that years ago."

"You never said anything."

"I figured if you wanted to talk about it, you would. That losing access to your young daughters was an emotional subject for you."

"Moreno was simply a wanna be gang leader when I first encountered him. I busted him on a minor drug charge and he did time in the county lockup. After he got out, he harassed Jenny whenever she took the girls out for a walk or to the park."

"And she was afraid of him." Nick could picture the situation.

"When I couldn't convince him to leave her alone, she left and first went to Nebraska, where her parents were. Then later disappeared, after her parents died. She wanted to cut ties with me completely. I let her have her way. And I've been sorry for years."

"You couldn't do anything about Moreno?"

"He hadn't committed an actual crime. There were no stalking laws on the books then."

"You two do have a history."

Doug took a piece of paper from his pocket and handed it to Nick. It said, "I know where you are. I'm coming after you. This time you die." The message was in block letters, signed with a large cursive M.

"When did you get this?" Nick couldn't keep the frustration out of his tone.

"I found it on my desk this morning. Meagan said a courier delivered it yesterday, while I was busy with everything else going on."

"This fits in with the text message I got today. The one I haven't had a chance to tell you about."

"What did it say."

"Velasquez said Moreno was ready to expand into the north-west, and he's planning to supervise the building of his business up here."

"So killing me is only part of his plan."

"That's the way I see it." Nick grimaced. "Going forward, you're the one we'll be protecting."

The door opened and a doctor in scrubs entered the room.

CHAPTER 27

Tricia moaned and forced her eyes open. Sharp pains pounded the side of her head. She was dizzy and disoriented. Moving only her eyes, she saw an IV. Saw a railing. Heard a monitor buzzing. She was in a hospital bed. Nick leaned over the bed, grinning widely.

"You've been out a long time. They kept you heavily sedated overnight. It's Friday morning." His clothes were rumpled, as if he'd slept in them. Blood stained his shirt. His? Or hers?

Daylight streamed in through the open blinds. "What happened." Her voice was weak and shaky.

"My shot hit Mobley. His shot grazed the side of your head. You have stitches."

"No wonder my head hurts, inside and out." Then she moaned from the effort of talking.

"That was a risky move you made." He grimaced. "You could have been killed."

"I couldn't let him take me out that door." She closed her eyes. Sleep tried to overtake her, but the pounding pain jolted her awake. She slowly opened her eyes. Nick was bending over her, watching her closely.

"Is he dead?" She squeaked out the words.

"Very dead."

"Thanks. You saved my life."

"It's a good thing I got down there in time." He reached out and grasped her hand.

Comforting. Her eyes closed. She forced them open. "I saw you over there, but so did Mobley. I needed to get out of the way. I didn't get far enough from the gun, I guess." A moan escaped.

"Don't try to talk anymore. You'll be okay."

Despite the pain, she had questions. "Alison? Did he hurt her?"

"He tied her up. Locked her in a closet. She was lucky he was focused on getting to you quickly."

She sighed. "I was worried about her, that he'd killed her too."

"Luckily he didn't. And he won't ever hurt anyone else."

She shifted on the bed, and a bolt of pain shot through her skull. She winced.

"Lie still."

"I'm stiff and sore where he jerked my arms around."

"You had cuts on your feet too, from going down the stairs without shoes."

"That's why they're stinging."

Her eyes wanted to close, but she was too thirsty to fall asleep. Rotating her head slightly, ignoring the pain, she saw the cup with a straw on the table to her side. She reached out, but misjudged the distance and knocked over the plastic cup, spilling the precious water on the table and the floor.

"You could have asked me to get it for you. Is it too much for you to admit you need help? Need someone?"

She gazed at him, her mouth open. But no words came out. Is that why she resented him being here, protecting her? Yes, if she were truthful. Deep deep down inside, in that little part of her psyche she didn't like to examine. Her beloved independence had been the cause of her resentment. The independence that would make her grow old alone, if she didn't change. But could she change?

Nick retrieved the cup before it rolled on the floor, and refilled it with water from a pitcher on the cabinet. Then he raised the head of her bed so she was upright enough that she could sip the water. He brought the cup to her lips and she eagerly gulped down a few swallows then pulled away. "Thank you."

"You're welcome." He replaced the cup on the tray. "Doug is out in the hallway, waiting to see you. He wasn't happy about what you did."

"Mobley rammed the gun against my skull. It hurt. I had no choice." A moan escaped.

"I'll get Doug."

He walked out the door. A sinking feeling enveloped her. When would he leave town? Would he stick around long enough for her to get out of the hospital? Or would he bolt immediately, so she couldn't hurt him again?

The door opened, and Doug limped in, looking as rumpled as Nick. "You took an awful chance." Softly spoken words.

She breathed in as deeply as she could despite the pain. Talking to him wouldn't be easy. Nick and Doug were both so protective and thought they had all the answers. "That was cold steel pressing into my temple. I dropped down to break the contact. I knew Nick was there and would get him. It worked."

"And you got hit. The bullet could have gone in instead of grazed the side of your head." He reached out and touched her scalp, close to the bandage. "That was a nasty gash."

"But the bullet didn't go in." She kept her gaze steady.

"No, it didn't. You have another chance. At life. And what about Nick?"

"Isn't he going back to Los Angeles?"

"Did he say so? Did you two talk about it?"

She sighed. "No. We haven't had a chance to talk about anything other than what happened."

"I stayed out in the hall."

That sinking feeling resurfaced. "I think it's too late. Why would he trust me?"

"Because you trusted him?"

"I did, didn't I?" She'd trusted him to shoot Mobley for her. They'd all been there for her. Nick. Doug. The other agency employees. The police. The detective. The FBI. It hit her then, like another blow to the head. She got it. Her independence could have gotten her killed.

"I went into the restroom alone. I was upset. I'd quit my job before Talbot could fire me."

"I know. I'm sorry."

"I could have been killed because of my own stupidity."

"But you trusted when it counted."

She shifted on the bed and another stab of pain coursed through her head. "What's Nick going to do? Is he ready to leave?" She managed to get the words out, despite the pain.

"It's up to you, and him, to decide."

Her spirits rose. "When can I get out of here?"

"The doctor said they'd keep you for another night, for observation. And send you home tomorrow if you check out okay. How do you feel?"

"Like a bulldozer ran over my head. An excruciating headache. Probably normal with a head injury. I've never been shot before. I'm sure I've had medication to help the pain. I'm very sleepy."

"I'll go and let you sleep. I have things I have to do today. You get lots of rest, and I'll pick you up tomorrow morning." He smiled at her, a soft, caring smile. Then he left, closing the door behind him.

She let her eyes drift shut. Would Nick stay around? Did she want permanent with him? Yes. If he wanted her too. If he'd trust her to stay with him.

TRICIA SAT at the breakfast bar, eating a sandwich. The front door opened. And closed. Panic gripped her. She dropped her sandwich onto her plate.

"I'll go check." Alison left the kitchen.

She'd been home a couple of hours and still felt unsteady. Still felt the effects of the pain medication. Doug had brought her home and left Alison with her so she wouldn't be alone.

Voices. Nick. Did he come after his belongings from the bedroom? Where did he sleep last night? Here or somewhere else? Questions without answers.

Nick came through the door, Alison behind him. "Up and around, I see. How are you feeling?" He was carrying a bouquet of red roses in a lovely crystal vase.

"Like I was shot."

Nick laughed, but a forced laugh, like it seemed to be the required response. He set the vase on the end of the breakfast bar.

"Thanks for the roses." Was he as nervous as she was? "Have you had lunch?"

"No. But I know where the food is." He pulled open the door and grabbed the ham and cheese from the refrigerator.

Alison finished her sandwich. "I'm going to butt out and let you two have privacy. If you need me, Tricia, give me a call."

"Uh, okay." She saw the looks that passed between Nick and Alison. They'd discussed her leaving. Anticipation built inside Tricia. Her entire future hinged on what would happen today, what would be said, what decisions would be made.

Alison left, the front door snapping shut behind her.

Nick finished making his sandwich and sat down at the breakfast bar, in the place vacated by Alison.

"Someone refilled the refrigerator while you were in the hospital. A fresh deli chicken and fresh salads to go with the sandwich makings."

"I could get too used to that kind of service." She grinned. "Someone restocking the refrigerator when I'm out."

"Uh, what if I took on the job?" Nick's expression also asked the question.

She gazed into his eyes and saw something there that surprised her. A vulnerability that hadn't been there before.

Her heart rate accelerated. "So, what are you saying? That there's a chance you might stay in Portland?"

"I've considered it."

"I may need someone around to keep me out of trouble."

"You would give up your complete independence?"

"I've considered it."

He set down his sandwich. "That will take courage. A trait I admire in a woman."

She pushed aside her plate, no longer hungry. That vulnerability in Nick's eyes drew her in. "I discovered something about you. I can trust you to be there for me." She kept her gaze on his.

He seemed to hesitate, then his expression changed. It softened, if you could say that about a man.

"I love you. I don't think I ever stopped loving you. No other woman ever measured up." Sincerity came through his voice.

Her heart swelled and beat a staccato rhythm against her ribs. "And I never stopped loving you."

He caught her hand and cradled it gently. "Is Los Angeles a speed bump for you?'

"Do you mean would I go there to be with you?"

"And don't say you'd consider it."

"You're testing the strength of my love for you?"

He sighed. "I'm being unfair. Oh, hell. I quit my job on Monday. I don't have a job to go back to. I want to stay in Portland with you."

Her jaw dropped and she gazed at him, processing what he'd said. "You quit the job you loved?"

"I was ordered to fly back Monday night and report to work Tuesday morning. I couldn't leave you unprotected."

"That's what that telephone call was about. The anger I heard in your voice."

"Yes."

"You quit the job you loved for me." Her brain attempted to sort out the ramifications. What would have happened had he left? Tears tried to push their way out.

He must have realized she was on the verge of crying. He jumped up and reached for her. She slid from the stool into his arms. And his lips descended on hers, gently, probing, sensual. Sending tingling sensations soaring through her body. Confirming what she already felt deep down in her bones, that she could not do without this man.

He ended the kiss and gazed at her. "This is what I want. You in my arms."

"For how long?" Her eyes searched his, for any hidden meaning. Finding nothing but sincerity and that interesting vulnerability.

"Will eternity do?"

A sudden whoosh of emotion hit her. A sudden breathlessness. Eternity? That ought to be long enough to drink in the scent of this man, enjoy his lovemaking. "Eternity would be nice. Is that what you're offering me?"

"I'm offering marriage. Will you marry me? Will you have my children?"

That stopped her for a moment. She hadn't thought much about a family, but she'd miss having kids and grandkids if she didn't act soon. Her biological clock was running down. She was thirty-two. "I was an only child. You had one sister. I'm thinking plural too. Children."

He tightened his grip on her.

She smiled at him. "I like that. Yes, I'll marry you. Marriage has to be a part of any package that includes children, for me."

"For me too."

"Will you be able to find a job here?"

He sat down and pulled her onto his lap. "I filled out an application for a job in Portland. Chet wants me in the division."

"Is Portland enough of a home to you?"

"My dad was a cop here. I grew up here. Yes, it's home. And you're here."

"I don't have a job anymore. I quit."

"You can find another job, if you want one."

"Or not. We can get started on our family. And renegotiate the job situation later."

"I like that term—negotiate. I think we'll work real good as a team, in a marriage."

"I like the way you think." She leaned toward him, pressing her lips to his. No longer able to resist the allure of the man she loved.

AUTHOR'S NOTE

Thank you for buying Dare to Resist! I hope you enjoyed it. This book is number one in the Those Who Dare series. All the books in this extended series are connected to Landreth Investigations in Portland, Oregon. Books two and three will be out soon. Their titles are Dare to Challenge and Dare to Conquer. Watch my website for more details.

http://barbararaerobinson.com

You can also subscribe to my newsletter on any page of my website and receive advance notice of future publications in the series or future books.

If you liked the book, please let other readers know by writing a review and posting it on the site where you purchased the book. Thanks!

ABOUT THE AUTHOR

Barbara Rae Robinson writes romantic suspense novels that sizzle with the heart-pounding rush of danger and the edgy emotions of falling in love. After her debut romance with Harlequin, Barbara turned her attention to combining romance with suspense. Her current project is an ongoing series of tales of death-defying heroic men and courageous women. Barbara lives in rural Oregon, close to Portland, the setting of her current series.

http://barbararaerobinson.com

facebook.com/barbararae.robinson
twitter.com/Barb_Robinson

www.ingramcontent.com/pod-product-compliance
Lightning Source LLC
Chambersburg PA
CBHW020404210626
46816CB00006BB/2114